Customer Service Can Be Deadly

Book Two in the Customer Service Can be Murder Series

Chris Pierce

Kindle Edition

Copyright 2018, Christine Pierce

To hear about new books and book sales, please sign up for my mailing list at:

http://www.niche-publications.com/contact/

I will not spam you or pester you but I will send you a link when the next book in the Customer Services Can Be: series is available on sale, and whenever I have a free promotion!

Dedication

This book is dedicated to my amazing family in all its extended glory—

I need to make specific mention of my beautiful daughter, who is no longer in China and whose three kids keep me young.

My adventurous son, who is now in New York with an amazing wife and new son.

And, of course, my geek-for-a-husband, who really does think a little kiss and cuddle will cure anything. You are my heart!

I also want to dedicate this book to my mom and dad who believed in me my whole life!

You are what you eat, so DON'T be fast, easy, or cheap.

—Anonymous

Contents

Chapter One

A Walk on the Cold Side

A pale man in a grey jogging suit stood at the end of driveway in the subzero wind. I was leaning into the wind and getting blown around fighting just to get to my car.

"I need your help," he said.

Oh, no, not again, was all I could think.

"How?" I realized I asked it out loud.

"Car," he replied. "It's almost a mile."

"Is this going to make me late for work?" I asked, opening the passenger door of the car. He hesitated and then slowly slid into the passenger seat.

"I'm a pretty good driver," I quipped, thinking he must be afraid of cars. I've met some survivors of accidents who avoid them as much as possible.

My old, reliable Saturn started on the first turn of the ignition with just a little whirring before it caught. I breathed a sigh of relief as the heater threw cold air on us and I knew it was working. It was still set to defrost from yesterday so I gave the wipers a swipe to make sure they were not frozen and looked over with my eyebrows raised.

"Which way?" I asked. He pointed left.

"Okay, Baby," I murmured patting the dashboard. "No dying and making me walk today."

No comment from the car but her engine kept blowing cold air on us. I twisted awkwardly to look both ways due to my bulky winter coat. My parka was a funny pale blue or blue-grey color from its many washings, but it was huge and filled with down substitute and very warm. It is my go-to coat for below zero weather. But it is very hard to see anywhere but straight forward because it puffs up over my shoulders and the hood wants to come down over my eyes to my nose. When it's just cold and not below zero, I usually take it off to drive and throw it in the backseat, but not this morning. It was still too cold to take off even my gloves.

It was hard to see through the frosted window so I turned to the man and asked him, "So, my name is Christine McCullum. I feel like I know you after you helped me this fall but I don't even know your name. What is it?"

"Call me Guy."

"Is that your name?"

"No. We really need to get moving. This is life or death."

I sighed, opened the frosty driver's window and started down the driveway. I went slowly and luck was with me. No one was coming either way. Gunning it, we started left with my head half out the window to see as the windshield was still frosted up and would be for at least fifteen minutes.

We only went three-quarters of a mile when Guy said, "Stop here."

It was the public access to our lake and the road was deserted. I stopped the car and got out, leaving the car running. The chance of a car thief being out and waiting for me to leave the car unlocked was real low. I have the opinion that thieves are a bit lazy and waiting in subzero weather is no job for a slug.

"Okay," I said through the slit between my parka hood and the collar. "What's so important?"

There was no answer. He was no longer in my car or anywhere I could see. Wonderful, I thought to myself. Just wonderful. He said it was a matter of life and death, I guessed I could look around.

It was still dark and the wind was kicking up swirls of snow on the frozen lake. The ice houses looked empty and cold. Ice fishing is big in Minnesota and many people even go out on lakes within the city limits. By the end of the season we will have little clusters of ice houses looking like villages from another world. But today, they were empty and silent. All I heard was the wind, and all I could see were ghostly wind-devils of snow.

Except one that seemed to have a shadow in it. As I watched, it didn't dissipate.

Would it be stupid to wander out on the lake in this wind? Yes, it would. There was no way I'd fall in, as the ice was strong enough to drive a car over, but it was wide open and the wind was extremely cold today. If there was a chance someone was in trouble would I be able to live with the guilt of not checking? The answer was no. I grew up Lutheran and we have very well-developed guilt.

With a sigh of frustration, I grabbed my extra scarf from the back seat and wrapped it around my neck, covering my mouth and nose. It takes just a minute to get frostbite in this weather and fingers, toes, and noses can be damaged beyond repair in five minutes of exposure. Frostnip just itches and is annoying for weeks but frostbite can be dangerous and frozen fingers, toes, or even feet can become useless for life.

In my heavy boots and full parka I was fine, but a walk in the wind was still not my first choice to start the day. The snow squeaked under my feet as it does only in subzero weather and the sound itself sent shivers down my back.

I headed for the shadow and walked as carefully and quickly as I could. It's easy to fall on windswept ice. To my horror I saw I was right. There was a woman in trouble out there, dressed in a cheap coat and hair blowing around her face. She was stumbling and seemed to not know what direction she wanted to go.

I hurried to her and turned her to face me. She couldn't seem to focus on my face. I opened my parka and pulled her into me, pressing her to my warmth. She mumbled something but I couldn't understand. Closing my huge coat around both of us, I walked her back to the shore and my car. I sat in the back seat and pulled her in with me.

She started to shiver uncontrollably. Good, that was better than before but hypothermia was beyond my skill. I reached around and dug in my purse, pulling out my cell phone. I dialed 911 and requested assistance.

The first responders got a name out of the lost lady, Beth Sanders, and told me that they were taking her to the county hospital. Exposure is not something you mess with in this frozen part of the world. They asked for my contact information and asked if it was okay with me to share with Beth if she asked. I agreed—I wanted to know that she was better. A phone call was all I expected. I was a few minutes late to work but I planned to be at least half an hour early so no one knew or cared. I was looking forward to putting this morning behind me.

We had a few call-ins but that was expected as those who use the bus are not always willing to wait in the cold when it dips far below zero. I work at a call center as a supervisor and my team dispatches engineers out into the field for mainframe repair and we also help the field engineers with their smartphones.

We have an assortment of interesting people working customer service over the phone and it's a good thing. When your office is full of unique—and occasionally odd—people, you have a lot of practice at rolling with the unique calls that come in. For example, we have engineers from all over the country calling in for help and sometimes it can be a little too personal. One time during the late shift I had to wake an engineer to replace parts on a computer at an airport. He sounded vague and then there were crashes and then he calmly told me, no worries, just fell down the stairs. Being unique and varied helps us with the interactions we have in the customer service role. We have to be able to roll with the situation, which is all I really did by listening to my stalker. He may be weird, but I expect my people to deal with weird, so more weird is not impossible to understand.

We have a bay of cubicles that clusters around my desk. Each cubicle has a phone with a headset and a monitor that is routed through a bank of mainframes somewhere out East. The calls come through many different 800 numbers, each number indicating a contract or a project. The mainframe has a logging system that allows my people to see who is calling and what services they contracted us to do. The field engineers can be pulled up by their employee numbers and we can see where they are and what they are doing, usually. I'm always astounded by how well the data is handled. A couple of my people claim it's all magic. Some call it "technomagic." For that reason, none of us are surprised when it doesn't work right and something goes haywire or wonky. That's why they still need us lowly humans.

There weren't enough customer service catastrophes to keep my mind off this morning. I don't know if there could be enough distractions to keep my mind off this morning. I called the county hospital at noon and asked how Beth Sanders was doing and if she could take visitors. They said she could take visitors but was due to be released before the end of day. I decided to take a chance on seeing her on the way home. Not a good gamble, it turned out.

Chapter Two

Visitors After Dark

Beth was not at the hospital. "She's been released," is all they would tell me. I headed home discouraged. It's nice to have an ending to such a dramatic story and I wanted to see her all better.

My kids are off finding themselves, so there was only myself, my cat and my husband to fill our huge house. My husband, Kristoffer, was not home when I got there and I was not surprised. He is a sweet geek who understands computers better than people and works more hours than most people stay awake.

Ever since my neighbor had issues with her ex-husband, I've been locking up religiously and we added lights along the driveway. I didn't take any extra time getting into the house. The wind had calmed down a little but it was still below zero. That kind of cold makes the bones hurt and ache.

That is why I was surprised when my doorbell rang twenty minutes later. Not likely a package being delivered so late, and not a door-to-door salesman. I peeked out the window on my front door and there was Beth. I let her in quickly closing the door on the wind.

"Hi!" I said. "Are you ok?"

She nodded, then shook her head, then shrugged.

"Humm," I replied. "Would you like tea?"

She nodded and followed me to the kitchen, not taking off her coat or her mittens. I watched her standing there as I put a few mugs in the microwave to heat the water.

"I've become fond of peppermint tea with honey," I said.

She nodded.

"Please sit, relax," I murmured. She was so uncomfortable it was making me uncomfortable. And this was my house, my kitchen. I should not feel awkward in my own kitchen. "Take off your mittens and coat and sit down."

"Need help," she croaked nervously as she held out a mittened hand. I started to reach for it and she said, "Gently, please."

I nodded and very slowly drew the mitten off a completely wrapped hand. "Oh, no," I whispered, helping her with the other mitten and her coat. "Are you going to lose any fingers?"

"They said no," she replied, still in a hoarse voice, "but I have blisters and it's quite uncomfortable."

"You're lucky," I said, "Can you handle a cup?"

"I'm lucky because of you," she replied. "I was lost and I don't even remember how I got on the lake or what I was doing."

The microwave dinged and I put tea bags and several teaspoons of honey in each cup, stirring them as the tea brewed.

"You don't remember anything?" I put the cups on the table. "Be careful it's hot."

"No, but the cops are telling me all kinds of things. I'm really scared," She picked up the cup with both hands and blew on it. She smiled and smelled the steam, "Nice. Thank you."

I nodded and decided to enjoy my tea and wait for the story. It was how I got most of the information I needed from my employees. It's amazing what people will say if you listen and let them talk.

Five minutes went by and she just occasionally smiled at me through the steam and seemed to be lost in the sensory enjoyment of a cup of tea.

I waited. Finally, she looked at me again and said, "They gave me monster pain meds."

I nodded wondering what I was going to do with her. She shouldn't be driving on pain meds and she shouldn't be walking in this cold. I knew nothing but her name. I was feeling the same way I had when Sally's ex-husband was terrorizing her. I was scared of something happening to her and spending my life in guilt. I have a well-developed sense of guilt. I also didn't want to sit around thinking about what could be happening. I have a very vivid imagination.

"Beth?" I said.

She was looking around the kitchen.

"Beth," I repeated. "Why are you here? What can I do to help?"

"I don't remember. Can I take a nap?"

"Can I take you home?"

"Nope, cops said not to go home."

"Why?"

She shrugged. "I'm not sure, they weren't making any sense. My husband murdered—"

She smiled blankly at me and I shivered. This was macabre.

"Your husband murdered . . .?" I repeated as a question, re-thinking my decision to invite her in. But it was way too late and too cold to leave someone on the doorstep with nowhere to go.

Her smile was secretive and feral, and she kept talking.

"He can't be murdered. You can't kill Evil, it just comes back angry." She shook her head. "No, he wasn't murdered, he's just toying with them."

She stood up, walked into the living room, laid down on the couch and immediately fell asleep.

I stared at her for a minute. I didn't think of myself as sheltered or naïve. But did I just let a crazy person in to sleep on my couch?

Chapter Three

Brandy and the Police

My best friend and neighbor, Mindy, made the trek across the road because I called her and told her I would hurt her if she didn't. I needed to talk to someone who made sense, even if just for a few minutes.

"You promised hot toddies and chocolate," she grumbled as she stomped her feet to make sure they weren't numb and threw her wool coat on the rack.

I also bribed her.

"I have a little problem," I admitted.

"No brandy?"

"No," I replied. "I have a guest and I don't really know why."

She looked over at my couch. "Is that Beth?"

"You know her?"

"She's come to the shelter where I volunteer several times. She never stays."

"Humm," I replied pensively. "What is her story?"

"Tragic tale of woe, as Shakespeare would say."

"What?"

"Abuse, but she wouldn't press charges and she always went back." Mindy sighed and started some tea herself. "Where's the brandy?" she asked, looking at my liquor shelf.

"On the counter," I replied. "That's it? Don't you have more of a story than that?"

"What do you want? It's the oldest story in my book. Pitiful in my opinion but who cares about my opinion?"

"The judge and jury," I quipped, teasing her.

"Not too bloody often," she replied.

"Well this one seems to have developed a twist." I said joining her for a hot toddy. I put several tablespoons of honey in mine. "Seems she was told not to go home because her husband was murdered."

"Really?" Mindy put down her cup and went to the cupboard for a treat to go with the wonderful, warm drink.

"You don't seem very surprised."

"Oh, honey," she replied with a fake sweetness. "You are so sweet and sheltered."

"Oh, yeah, you big, bad lawyer. Suing all those nasty husbands."

"It's a job," she replied. "Look, most women's shelters are funded by the police or other law organizations because so many of the abusive situations end in the final violence. If he doesn't kill her, she kills him."

"What?"

"It's in the numbers."

I looked over at the exhausted woman sleeping so peacefully on my couch. "So . . . you think she killed her husband?"

"It's better than likely."

"No evidence, nothing. Just, 'The wife did it'?"

Mindy laughed, "No one cares what we think. What did she say?"

"Beth doesn't believe he's dead. She said, 'Evil can't be killed.' "

"I don't think you should keep her here."

"You saying she's off her rocker?"

"Yup."

"Mindy," I said, trying to get her to pay attention to me. "I'm open for suggestions. What should I do with her? I don't feel much like going to bed and leaving her there."

"I highly doubt you're in danger," Mindy said, matter-of-factly.

"Highly doubt?" I repeated.

"Yeah, I don't think she'll be violent towards you. And she might not ever remember what happened."

"You are a ray of sunshine," I retorted.

Mindy shrugged. "I try not to get too involved," she explained. "Victims of abuse can drag you down to their private hell if you let them."

"So you just shrug and drink doctored tea?"

"Hang on there," Mindy retorted almost as if I insulted her. "I work at the shelter and I do pro bono work. Do you?"

"No."

"What do you do to help?"

"I don't know what I can do. It's not like I can customer service them out of trouble."

"Not being able to help is a problem all right. The shelter can help. A few find their way out." She added more brandy to her tea. "You could volunteer at the shelter, you know. They need kitchen help and house cleaning, and—"

"Shut up," I snapped and started to laugh at her. She knows what a poor housekeeper I am. My cooking is okay, so long as you can handle lots of wine and brandy as those are my two favorite ingredients.

The wind blew outside and the windows rattled. "Well, this is a fine kettle we're in," I said. "Too cold to send her on along by herself and I'm too drunk to take her anywhere."

"Maybe you will have to keep her," Mindy replied, giggling. This was a mess. Both of us were too many sheets to the wind to make a good decision or act on one if it jumped up and screamed. "Why is she here anyway?"

"I saw her wandering on the lake before sunrise and got her to the paramedics."

"Saved her, huh?"

"Guess so."

"What was she doing wandering around in this weather in the dark?"

"She didn't remember and she was really disoriented."

Mindy just shook her head. Finally, she seemed to have an idea make it through the fog. "Tell you what," she said. "Tomorrow I'll help you get her situated at the shelter until this is straightened out."

"What is straightened out?"

"That's part of the problem, right? We don't know."

I nodded, and the doorbell rang again. I looked at it and decided it had to go. It was just way too chipper and active a doorbell.

It rang for the third time that night, and I wandered over to silence it. Two large policemen stood at my front door flashing badges at me.

"What can I do for you?" I asked.

"First, we need you to invite us in," the older of the two replied.

"Okay, come in," I responded stepping backwards.

They came in and walked over to Beth, waking her and telling her about her rights at the same time.

"Help me," she whispered looking at me. Her eyes were wide and her face pale.

I started to move towards them but Mindy held my arm. "Wait," she said quietly.

As they were starting to head back to the front door, Mindy stepped forward.

"Gentlemen, may I have a word with my client?"

"You a lawyer or something?" the younger officer asked. I decided he wasn't the brains of the twosome.

"Yes, I am," she replied.

They tracked wet into my kitchen, leaving Beth with Mindy but watching. "Going to offer us some tea or coffee?" asked the older and apparently more polite of the two.

"No, not right now," I replied. "I don't understand. What are you arresting Beth for? She is obviously a victim here."

"We can't discuss anything with you ma'am," he returned.

"Gentlemen," Mindy said walking into the kitchen with an air of calm that I knew was reserved for people she didn't like. "Please make sure Beth gets medical attention again tonight and please keep her safe."

They escorted Beth out and I bolted the door behind them. I turned to Mindy, "You're her lawyer?"

"I am now, at least until I find someone more qualified. I am not a criminal attorney."

"But, you think she's guilty."

"So it's an even better idea to get a more qualified attorney."

I dumped out my tea and poured straight brandy into my cup. "And," I challenged. "How did they know she was here?"

"When they were questioning Beth at the hospital, she said she wanted to talk to the lady who pulled her off the lake and say thank you. She said they ignored her and she thought they were done so she got up and walked here, it's only a mile or so. They must have had to think a long time to figure it out. I wonder how long it took for them to notice."

"Ouch," I laughed. "You are not being supportive of our men in blue there."

"They're a mixed lot and most of them very reasonable. It's just that it usually is the wife or the husband and I think they get tired of it." She took my cup and slammed the rest of my brandy. "In fact, so do I."

Chapter Four

A Matter of Trust

Morning found me no longer alone. I had a snoring husband next to me and an alarm ringing. I turned it off as quickly as I could, not knowing what time he came home. It was long after I went to sleep. He mumbled something and turned over, stopping the snoring.

"Good morning to you, too," I laughed and slapped his butt. Fun to tease when he's too out of it to do anything about it.

He smiled in his sleep and I grinned knowing that I gave him good dreams if nothing else.

We keep our house at 68 degrees at night and 72 during the day. There are thermostats that warm the house up before you get up. We don't have one of those.

I dressed quickly and in layers, several soft undershirts and a huge sweater. It's good to be prepared. I made a coffee to go and noticed fruit on the side table. Awesome, he bought fruit. I snagged an apple and an orange and threw it in my bag. Now, I was prepared for anything.

It was still cold between my car and my house and the snow still squeaked when I stepped on it. But the wind had stayed away and the sun was coming up bright. I pulled on my sunglasses before starting the car. I don't know why but a sunny day on snow and in subzero temperatures is exceptionally bright, and the first few miles of my trip to work is directly into the sunrise.

It was quiet when I arrived. I'm usually first to arrive of the day shift because I like to see the third shifters before their shift is done. I talked to each one of them and then I was interrupted by a call from Mindy.

"I talked to Beth this morning at the courthouse," she said without preamble.

"Good morning!" I chirped. I was in full Supervisor Mode.

"Right," she replied dryly. "Seems her husband had some money and she doesn't need to use the free court appointed defense. That's the good news. The bad news is that she was booked and processed. They believe they have a good case for first-degree murder."

"What does Beth say? Is she making any sense this morning?"

"She's in pain as they haven't approved her pain meds in lockup, but she is less dazed. She still doesn't remember much, just snaps of being terrified and cold. You really did save her life, you know?"

"Wonderful, just in time for her to be arrested for murder."

"The high-powered attorney she hired is very good and very busy." Mindy continued. "He often hires out secondary investigative work and he has asked me to coordinate this. It pays well so I'm going to do it."

"Good," I said with a sigh of relief. "Now someone will watch out for her interests."

"Well, I'm pretty busy with my own case load. And we need a licensed PI if we want our information to be taken seriously. And honestly, if we want to find the real scoop."

"Good plan," I agreed. "She needs an independent to look out for her interests."

"She told the attorney that she only trusts you," Mindy countered. "That means we need to get you working for the firm."

"What?" I squeaked. "I don't know the first thing about what to do."

"He'll tell us what he wants us to find out. And I contacted a PI firm. They are willing to take you on as an intern with no pay as I made it a condition to using them but you have to do everything they say and how they say."

"Why me?"

"Beth has requested you be involved. Now that she isn't so drugged, she is feeling pretty paranoid and fearful that no one cares if she did it and how it affects her. She trusts you. And right now, only you."

"Jeez," I mumbled. "What did I do to get involved in this mess?" Oh yeah, I remember—that skinny guy who wants to be called Guy because he doesn't want me to know his name! Yeah, that personal stalker of mine, who told me she needed help and disappeared. Just wait until I get my hands on him!

"We can start by figuring out the story of who her husband was and if he had any enemies," Mindy continued through the phone as if she hadn't lost me.

"Oh, great." I mumbled. "You want me asking questions?"

"No," Mindy snapped. "Quiet research. Keep track of the time you spend."

I'm doing the work and some PI will be paid?

"Where?" I asked, my head starting to hurt. "At the library?"

"His full name is Ben Richard Sanders and he was a contractor with a real estate license. I'd start on the internet if I had time."

"Come over tonight after work and make me supper," I replied vaguely. "We'll talk."

I figured that would be the end of it because Mindy hated to cook. I misjudged her resourcefulness. She arrived at my house that evening with Thai takeout that smelled very spicy with curry overtones. Yumm was all my brain wanted to say.

I will admit, I can be bribed.

But, I'm still not a PI. I didn't have even a clue what I should be doing. "Mindy, listen," I started reasonably. "I can't help."

"Sure you can," she replied. "We just need to do background research and be involved so Beth trusts her attorney and his team."

"By we, do you mean me?"

"Yes."

I booted up my laptop computer in the kitchen.

"Why do they think it was Beth?"

"She had motive—he was hurting her. She had opportunity, she can't account where she was. She can't prove she wasn't there."

"Motive and opportunity can't be the only steps to damning a person to prison," I returned.

"No, of course not. But, right now she is the only suspect they are pursuing because they believe she did it."

"Why?"

"Let's not get into the numbers again, it usually is the spouse. Another reason they believe it was her is that it was done with her kitchen knife and her fingerprints are on the handle. It was very messy and very personal."

"Then why wasn't she covered with blood?"

"What?"

"She was wandering around on the lake before dawn. I pulled her into my coat, I held her until the paramedics arrived. Why didn't I notice any blood? Why didn't it come off on me?"

"She cleaned up?"

"Right, she killed him, she was in shock, and for some reason she showered, then wandered out onto the lake?"

"Good point . . . are you sure no blood transferred to your clothes?"

"I haven't washed them yet, can they be tested?"

"Yes. I don't know if we can get them introduced as evidence, probably not. But we can push to have her clothes tested because you're right, she should have been a bloody mess if she murdered someone and that led to her wandering around with a break in her memory."

"How do I have them tested?"

"Humm, ask. Don't wash them. But, if they do have blood on them and you didn't notice, it will hurt her case."

"Can't worry about that. If we want to help we have to believe she might be innocent and convince others that she might not have done it."

"We have to worry about getting her off. Justice is a fickle mistress and we are not worried about her."

"Jeez, you're still such a ray of sunshine," I grumbled, grabbing the last spring roll.

I cleaned up my hands and returned to my computer with visions of quickly uncovering tons of personal information about Mr. and Mrs. Ben Richard Sanders.

The first search for background information on Ben Richard Sanders got six hits of groups who promised to tell me everything, with a modest monthly fee for the service. Then my virus checker clicked in and I had to reboot my computer.

It was becoming very clear to me that I not only didn't know enough to start, but I didn't know how to search for this type of information online either. I needed to know more personal information about both of them and I needed to know what I was looking for. Just searching blindly was really and truly shooting in the dark.

"Mindy," I said finally, "I need to talk to Beth and this lawyer."

She nodded. "Good plan," she said closing her phone and standing up. "Do you have a list of questions?"

"No," I replied, "But I will."

"This is the lawyer's number, you'll have to arrange with him to talk to Beth."

I walked her to the door, wondering what I managed to wander into and where I was going to find the time.

Chapter Five

No Answers but a Bloody Body

Morning found me with a bit of a hangover and an over-excited boss. It seems our company was contracted to install plasma televisions for a nationwide retailer. "Huge opportunity" and "unlimited potential" bounced around like balloons and became the words of the day. Forgive me for not feeling euphoria. This sounded like a different direction for our field engineers. Maybe it was the hangover talking.

I had every intention of dragging my sorry butt home and detoxing with a long bath and fancy water, but the firm of Doyle, Nelson, and Humphry called me just as I was leaving. Seems Mindy made a 4:30 appointment for us to meet with the PI firm and arrange for an interview. I'm not one for ignoring appointments and she knows it.

Muttering the entire way, I used MapQuest on my phone to get me to the office. Mindy was at the door, her coat blowing in the wind. I so wanted to just pounce on her that I almost went over the curb while parking.

"What the hell!" I said in way of greeting.

"Well aren't you Miss Customer Service this afternoon?" she responded.

"I don't want to be here; I have a headache and my job just exploded, and—" I didn't get to even start on my rant before she opened the door and the warm air wafted out.

Fine, ok, I'd go in and warm up first.

The office was impressive, with glass and chrome everywhere. A chipper security/secretary in a uniform walked us to a private room and a lean man in crisp slacks and neat blue golf shirt came in. He smiled and handed me a firm handshake. "I'm Josh Biten, an investigator on the defense for Beth Sanders," he said.

"Nice," I replied.

"Seems Beth is very scared and is insisting you be part of our investigation," he continued.

"That's what I heard," I replied brusquely. I was not feeling or acting very grown up at this point.

"Are you willing to be a part of our team and give her some confidence in us?"

I was silent and Beth elbowed me.

"Ow," I yelped, glaring at her.

"I understand you're interested in helping her," he said, smoothly ignoring my bad manners.

"I don't know much except customer service," I replied. "I seriously don't see how I can help. I want to help Beth but I don't have a clue what to do. I tried to use the internet to look up stuff and all it wants is for me to sign up for services and pay a lot of money."

He nodded and smiled with perfectly straight, white teeth. "I see you're smart enough to know it's not easy."

Okay, I'll admit it, a compliment after a day of nonsense was nice.

"All I know is how to talk to people," I replied.

"Really?" he quipped dryly with a little smile. His eyes gave away a good sense of humor and I realized I could probably work with this guy.

"Yeah, and sometimes I'm even nice."

"No need," he muttered.

"I would need to talk to Beth first, see what she thinks, and get more information about her husband and their life together. I would need to learn so much and I have a job and . . ." I petered out thinking about how little after work I really had to do these days with my kids off finding themselves.

"So, you're really a PI?" I blurted.

"I'm an investigator for a nationwide firm who specializes in research for attorneys for the defense."

"So yes!" I laughed. "And you have a license and a gun?"

"Yup," he replied, "but I have not had to use it 'cause I'm smart."

"The license or the gun?"

He didn't answer. He just got up and said, "We can go talk to Beth now, she's in holding and I have an appointment."

"Why hasn't she been released on bail?" I asked.

"That's a question for the attorney."

"And why wasn't she covered in blood?" I asked as we talked to the elevator. Mindy didn't come with us, she deserted me and went to her car with a little wave. I glared.

"Why would she be?" Josh asked, getting my attention back.

"If she killed her husband, close and personal with a knife, wouldn't there be blood on her and her clothing?"

"Not if she cleaned up."

"And then after cleaning up she chooses to go out into subzero temperatures before sunrise to damage her health?"

"Good point, but not enough to prove her innocence. We need to make sure the attorney for the defense is not surprised or uninformed. That's our job. I'll make sure the attorney has the clothes tested for blood and we have the results."

"Can you have the clothes I was wearing tested also?"

"Yup, probably can't prove they weren't washed. But it doesn't sound like Beth had a chance to wash hers."

We piled into a nondescript grey sedan and he drove to downtown holding.

We were able to see Beth in a small interview room. She looked much better to me, even in ugly prison garb. She had clear eyes and her hands were only sporting light bandages.

"Hello, Mr. Biten," she said formally, sounding like a woman who could afford a high-powered attorney.

She smiled shyly at me. "Are you really willing to join these guys and help me?"

"I guess, although I don't understand why you want me."

"I don't trust them and I don't want to tell a man anything. Please tell me you'll watch them and help me."

"I'll do what I can, but to find the truth you are going to have to talk to me."

"Not now, I can't."

"When?"

"I don't know."

"How about for now you just tell me your full name and social security number, and your husband's. And any business associates he may have had," I countered. "I want to do some background work and you wouldn't believe how many Beth Sanders are on the internet."

She nodded and whispered, "Come back tomorrow without him."

"Beth," I countered, changing track. "I can't do this unless you're honest. Did you kill your husband?"

"I don't think so," she replied. "I'm too scared of him to do that."

"You don't believe he's dead?" I asked, taken aback. "Don't they have to have a body to charge someone with murder?" I was confused. Did she believe she didn't kill anyone? Or did she believe someone else was killed?

"Beth," I said trying again. "Did you kill anyone?"

She shook her head, then shrugged. "I don't remember for sure what happened. I have strange flashes and they don't make sense."

"Why don't you believe he's dead?" I asked.

"Maybe this is a trick to make me say something. Maybe it isn't him?"

"Why would someone do that?"

She shook her head and wrapped her arms around herself.

Wonderful was my only thought. She sounded as sane as when she fell asleep on my couch. Maybe she was still confused and dazed.

On the drive back to my car, Josh was silent. Finally, just before I climbed out of his car, he turned to me.

"Can you meet me at the county courthouse tomorrow afternoon? I'll show you how to search some records physically and you can slip over to have a private chat with Beth. I'm not sure what she won't tell us but we need to make sure we know enough for a thorough report to the attorney. Surprises can kill a good defense. Make sure you say to her, 'This is a legal visit between Beth Sanders and myself, Christine McCullum. The matters we are to discuss are work product from her attorney's office and are not subject to being recorded, listened to, or monitored in any manner.' "

"Why the strange disclaimer?" I asked.

"It is to protect our clients from our conversations with them being used against them in a court of law. I don't usually accept help or trainees but she is paying a lot for our services and she wants you, and I think you can be an asset."

Why not? Sounded interesting and honestly all I had to go home to was an empty house and lazy cat. I nodded. "I can give you a couple of hours after work a couple days of the week."

My life had just changed. If I had known everything that was coming, would I have done it? Hard to say.

Chapter Six

Rumors and Pushback

Morning greeted me with flurries of fat snowflakes. This kind of snow is pretty and not usually very cold. I still dressed in layers but I added a festive sparkle in my hair using a barrette with a silver snowflake and bling. It was a little cheesy, but cheerful. I was determined to get the mood at work more positive and my team needed some attention.

Driving was slick but not backed up so I had time to slide into the bagel shop and get a couple dozen bagels and a couple tubs of cream cheese. "Feed the team" is an important mantra for me.

Gretchen flopped into the chair next to me with her bagel. She was my best lead and a very small woman. She also ate like six dock workers.

"How do you do that?" I asked pointing to the bagel half in her mouth. It was the third one I saw her eat but that didn't mean it was the last.

"What?" she asked, raising her eyebrows into her cap of soft, kinky black hair.

"Eat and stay so small. You have three kids."

"I can't afford to gain weight; all my clothes are this size."

"Whatever," I said, grinning. It was my fault for asking such a stupid question.

"Feel like listening?" she asked.

Now that was strange. I frowned at her.

"About what?"

"I heard a strange rumor."

Oh, no, was my only thought. This could be anything. I just raised my own eyebrows in question.

"Adeen told Billy he saw Gabriela working at Walmart." She smiled knowing she dropped a bomb of a rumor onto my head.

"I thought she was taken back to New Orleans on threats and maybe a murder charge," I said. She used to work on our team but told everyone during an ice breaker that she was scared of her son because she killed his dad. This caused all kinds of strange Human Resource issues because I could not fire her for something that was not proven in a court of law. It was a mess I would have liked to have forgotten about but because one of our team reported to the police that she was threatening him, and where she hid her gun, she was taken back to New Orleans for questioning about her ex's disappearance.

We didn't know it at the time, but at least being taken to New Orleans meant she missed enough work that I was able to terminate her for job abandonment. We thought it was over but apparently not, if she was back in town. The charges must not have been able to stick.

Gretchen shrugged. "That's what I thought, but I went to see for myself—she is working as a cashier at Walmart."

"Sure?" I muttered. I was not glad that she was back in town. There was never any evidence, but I was convinced she scared an employee into falling down the stairs. After Frank went to the police, he thought he heard breaking glass and fell down the stairs in the dark. How she scared him enough to fall down the stairs and start his decline I never could figure out. She was just not someone I would want to meet in a dark alley. Actually, I didn't want to meet her anywhere.

"Adeen said she told him they couldn't hold her on any charges. Said she smiled when she talked and it gave him the shivers."

"Did Adeen ask her about the charges?" I asked, surprised.

"Yup," Gretchen replied. "Adeen doesn't pull his punches." I guess not was my thought but I didn't say it.

"Well," I replied. "She's not my favorite person but she doesn't work here anymore and it's not our business."

"True, but I'd like to know more about her. She's up to something."

"Let's stick to what we need to know. Which brings me to a question: does your uncle still work for the sheriff's department in Scott county?" I asked, wondering if anyone was going to convince her to let it go, although I agreed with her bad feeling.

"Yup, he got his detective badge and is still chasing bad guys."

"Does he ever talk about work?"

"Nope, except to say mostly it's boring research and I should stay away from it. I have kids and I'm not married."

"What about the father of your kids?"

"I can't help who I love but I'm not marrying him."

I mentally shook my head. This was not my business and not what I wanted to talk about, so I effectively changed the subject.

"If I were to tell you that I'm going to do some research for a private investigative firm, what advice would you give me?"

"Don't tell my uncle or the cops, keep your head down, and stay off the streets at night."

Good advice that I should have followed.

Afternoon found me eager to get started. I took the leftover bagels and headed to the courthouse to meet with Josh.

He was glad to see the bagels and I discovered a similarity between the tall, lean blonde and my tiny, black lead. They both could consume more than their weight in bagels and cream cheese. Maybe I should go on a bagel diet, nothing but bagels and cream cheese. Seemed to work for them.

It turned out the actual courthouse is only open until 4:30 but Josh showed me how to use the webpages to check out property ownership and assessment values. As Beth's husband had a real estate license, Josh thought this might be a good direction to start.

Then I left Josh and went over to visit Beth.

It gets dark early in Minnesota in the winter and I parked on the street with the fat flakes of snow still falling and catching the light under the streetlights.

Josh would not have sent me downtown to visit Beth if it was dangerous. Right? I shivered and locked my car. I don't like dark cold streets.

"Talk to me," I said to Beth without preamble after the odd introduction Josh requested. I sat down across from her. She had put this off too long. Her eyes were clear and she looked like she was getting some sleep.

She shrugged. "What do you want to know?"

"Everything. Start with your full name, your husband's full name, social security numbers and anyone who didn't like your husband or you."

"Why do you need all that?"

"To search for you and him we need full names, and social security numbers, date of marriage and all that. To find a possible scenario other than you killing your husband in a fit of rage or self-protection, I need to know about him and your life."

She wrote down names and numbers on a piece of paper, and handed it to me.

"I trust you," she whispered. "But no one else."

"Talk to me," I repeated gentler. "Tell me about your life."

In customer service you learn that there is no stronger weapon than listening and empathizing with a customer or client. So, I prepared myself to listen. I was disappointed.

"He had a temper and would lash out," she started.

I nodded. I knew this.

"He always said sorry afterwards and explained why it was my fault."

I nodded. I guessed this.

"He made a good living and he and his partner did a lot of important real estate deals."

I nodded. I didn't know about a partner but I guessed that her expensive lawyer indicated there were some big deals.

"Can you tell me the name of his partner?" I asked. There was no mention of this anywhere I'd seen.

"Andy Butcher, I believe," she mumbled. "Andy for Andrew maybe, something like that. Andy was dating their girl I think."

"What do you mean, their girl?" I wondered aloud. My voice sounded loud to me as Beth seemed to always talk in mumbles or whispers. Maybe loud would help pull her out of her head.

"You know answer phones, do bookkeeping, that kind of stuff," she replied, still very quietly.

"And what was her name?" I prompted again, trying to use my voice to pull her into the here and now.

"Not sure, they just called her Our Girl."

Wonderful fellows these two.

"Now, will you tell him to stop teasing me and tell the cops he's not dead?" Beth whispered loudly. At least she was a little louder.

"I'm pretty sure he's dead. They don't bring charges of murder without a body."

"Are you sure?"

"Yeah, pretty sure."

She nodded and picked at her chipped nails. "Can you get me some nail polish?"

"Let's focus on keeping you out of jail before worrying about your nails. But, I'll ask. They searched me before we could talk so I'm sure they have a list of what is allowable."

She looked around. "Can we be done now?"

I didn't feel I'd gotten any real information from her but I did have full names and a new one even if it wasn't complete. Something to burn up on the internet tonight. I was also wondering if maybe fighting a murder charge should hold her interest over nail care. But, what did I know?

I bundled up and ventured back on the now completely dark street. The snow was coming down faster and it was getting colder. Why does it get colder so quickly when the sun goes down? My boots crunched on the snow-ice mix on the sidewalk and distant traffic was all I could hear.

My car was next to the parking meter with no other cars around and I was glad to see it under the streetlight. But, there was a shadow next to it and I stopped, wondering if it was safe. The wind blew and my scarf fluttered behind me. I needed to get into that car and away from here. The shadow moved and I saw a shape of a person facing me. Oh, no. I didn't know if I could outrun anyone and there was no one else around. Suddenly, the person turned and disappeared into the dark up the street. Someone just walking by, or messing with my car?

I hesitated, then got into my car quickly and started it up, locking the doors. When I turned on the wipers, a piece of paper was stuck under one. Great. Did I unlock the doors and get the paper or let it blow away? Silence was the only answer to my question and I sat in the cold car, shivering.

I don't deal well with fear. I will jump off a ski chair lift if it starts to swing as I would rather fall than be afraid. I opened the window quickly and grabbed the paper. I closed the window and relocked the doors, just to be safe.

Chapter Seven

Pepper Spray and Sex

I found my home, not dark and scary, but lit up and very welcoming! First thing I did was power up my computer and send a short note to Josh outlining my talk with Beth. I expressed my frustration with her state of mind and her not believing the victim to be her husband. Who else could it be? I didn't feel comfortable talking about the note on my windshield in email so I decided to talk to my husband first.

After hot soup and grilled cheese sandwiches I showed the note to Kristoffer.

His answer surprised me. "You shouldn't be touching it, in case the police could have gotten fingerprints, and you should keep it on a vision board to help motivate yourself."

Instead of appreciating his supportive attitude, it annoyed me. "You aren't worried about me?"

"What good would that do?" he asked innocently. "Would you stop? Would you blame me if you did?"

I stared at him. "How can you be so logical when I'm scared out of my bones?"

He handed me a bag from Micro Center. In it were several interesting boxes as well as a keychain with a tiny canister of pepper spray.

It made me feel warm all over that he would buy me pepper spray. But I had no intention of needing such a thing.

"How does it work?" I asked while turning it over. There was a button on the side.

"Not me!" he yelled, jumping away from me. Luckily, I only sprayed the wall. I examined the wall, coughing a little and wondering what removes pepper spray stains and smell. The entire hallway now smelled like jet fuel or a bad BBQ.

He started laughing like a loon and hugged me from behind. "Watch out, criminal element, you are about to be customer-serviced. You'll never be the same."

"You're making fun of me," I muttered, leaning back into him. "Does this toy come with refills?"

"In the bag," he whispered, nuzzling my neck and blowing air on the back of my neck.

The tiny hairs on my neck stood up and goose bumps appeared on my arms. I slid away and dumped the bag on our bed.

"Playing hard to get?" he asked as he swaggered up behind me.

"I think this whole situation turns you on."

"I always wanted to be married to Mata Hari."

"Who?" I laughed leaning back into him. "Didn't she die a terrible death?"

"Don't remember," he replied.

I turned to face him, "Tomorrow I'm going to 'do the neighborhood' with Josh."

"Josh?" he asked raising one eyebrow.

"Yup, he's the private eye hired by Beth's attorney. He thinks talking to neighbors is what I'll be good at."

"I'm sure you will be," he replied and nipped my nose. "Now stop talking."

Chapter Eight

Doing the Neighborhood

Morning was snowy but warmer. It was below freezing but above zero. The snow falling was pretty and almost fluffy.

After a day preparing for our new customer by learning a scheduling program that still had plenty of bugs, I really didn't want to go around with Josh. But he met me at work, honking his horn in the parking lot. Jeez, that was going to go over big with my employees. Now a new rumor would be circulating tomorrow. Oh well, I thought tossing on my coat and hat, it would amuse them. My husband would get a kick out of it if he heard, I hoped.

"Get moving, girlie," Josh quipped with a huge grin as I opened the door of his very boring grey sedan.

"You don't have to live up to a Private Dicks reputation," I snarled.

He flashed his white teeth at me. "Thanks for the specific information on Beth's husband and friends. It helps."

"Why can't I do the computer work and you do this legwork?" I asked, my voice scratchy and sounding grumpy even to me.

"Most of the databases are paid by the search and the good ones require a PI license to subscribe. Let me do the computer work. You get people to talk."

"With my winning personality?"

"Yup." He drove his gas-guzzler slowly out of the lot towards the upscale neighborhood on the other side of my lake.

"Why do you have such a boring looking car with an engine that growls with power and uses more gas than an airplane?"

"That's not true, Molly here does not use more gas than an airplane."

"You know what I mean," I said.

"You can probably guess, smart lady like yourself."

I didn't feel like guessing and I figured I knew. It was to keep a low profile but have lots of power. "Do we know without a shadow of a doubt that it was Ben Sanders killed?"

"What? Why would you ask?"

"Beth is so sure he isn't dead. How do they do the ID?"

"County morgue is doing a full autopsy. I'm pretty sure a positive identification is included."

"Just asking," I returned a little annoyed. "I'm not stupid."

"Not a bad idea to have the attorney raise the question. Could help the case. I'll pass it on."

He was starting to tick me off.

"Don't you want to know the truth?" I snapped.

"I want to help the attorney make sure Beth has a fair shot, and of course I want the truth. If we find evidence that helps the prosecution, we tell the attorney. He needs the truth as much as you want it if he's going to get Beth off."

Josh parked at a pretty park right on the lake. "We hoof it from here," he said. "Don't want to look like outsiders."

"And you don't want anyone seeing your car," I said.

He grinned at me. "Yup."

The first house was a pale blue and faced the frozen lake with its trees and walkways welcoming the frozen scene.

"Where are we compared to Beth's house?" I asked.

"This is it," he replied. "I want to walk through the crime scene as much as I can."

"I don't want to step over any closed-off crime scenes," I replied shaking my head.

"No, let's stay within the law today. Think of it as a field trip."

Funny guy.

There was a maze of footprints in the snow but the house was dark and silent with no indication it was ground zero. The front door was locked and no one answered the doorbell. Not surprising as Ben was dead and Beth was locked up.

"Anyone else live with them?" I asked.

"My question exactly," he said nodding. "No one answering the door does not answer the question unfortunately." He looked at me, "Write that down as a question to ask Beth on your next visit."

"Talking with her was a dead end."

"No, you got a new name to research and built on her trust. As long as she is in local holding and you can visit, I want you visiting at least once a week."

"Well, it was pretty scary leaving and finding a note on my car."

"Note? You didn't say anything about a note in your report."

"I didn't want to put it in writing. It seems so . . ." I shrugged and handed him the note in a baggie, both embarrassed and relieved to tell him.

He looked at it, looked back at me and looked at it again.

"Well, I'll be . . ." he said finally and I seriously considered screaming right there, in front of the house that had so recently seen real violence.

"She is less likely to be guilty if someone is threatening you into not talking to her. Someone must be watching the courthouse. Next visit, I'll follow you and try to catch the person watching. This will be fun." He actually grinned at me, showing his fine dentures. Excited was maybe the only reaction I wasn't expecting.

I shook my head. "I'm not a fighter."

"Not what I heard. Mindy asked me to take you on. I know Mindy from when she handled my wife's divorce, she's good. I did a complete background on you before agreeing. There was something in there about throwing a bottle of Merlot at a stalker."

"You're divorced?" That was all I got out of that.

"No, she was before I met her. Still freshly married, since you're asking," he replied playing his eyebrows up and down.

"Funny guy," I muttered and started walking around the house. The sun was sitting on the horizon and we had maybe an hour of light. I wanted to be home and soaking in rose water by dark.

Besides the attractive, pale blue color, this was a very nice two-story house. The landscaping plan was clear, even covered with snow. It separated the property and opened the yard to the lake. I nudged Josh and pointed to the footprints leading to the lake. It was not a single line as I almost expected but a mashed-up indication that multiple people walked or ran to the lake from the back door. Could have been the police or anyone actually. And it had been a few days, and at least one light flurry of snow.

He nodded and took pictures of the back-door latch. It was scratched a bit and could have been broken into. No proof it was. But for the police to prove only the accused had access to a locked house, the lock needed to be pristine and untouched. It being scuffed and scratched opened the door wider for a defense based on it being "some other dude'" who broke into the house.

We walked through the yard around the other side of the house and I admired the neat window treatments and the orderly garage.

A soft, "Hello," interrupted the silence. A small woman with a large dog was on the road watching us.

"Hi," I replied smiling. I noticed Josh backing away but she did not seem to.

"Do you live around here?" she asked.

"Nope," I replied. "Other side of the lake. About a mile up the hill."

She nodded, watching me and keeping her hand on the dog.

"Nice dog," I continued. "Can I pet him?"

"You can try," she shrugged. "He doesn't like anyone."

I hunkered down and held out my hand palm up and waited for him to respond to my invitation.

He tossed his head a few times and looked at his mistress for a clue. She didn't move and he stepped forward and sniffed my hand. I turned it over and he pushed into me, giving me his head to stoke. I scratched his ears and said soft words of praise and his tail wagged. He pushed into me again and I almost fell down laughing. I grew up with dogs and I missed having one all the time. My sweet husband could not handle any animal bigger than a cat due to his allergies.

She smiled at me.

"Do you know the Sanders?" I asked, hoping her dog's approval would be a factor in my favor.

"Why do you ask about my neighbors?" she countered.

"I'm working for Beth's attorney and asking questions about her and her husband."

She nodded and considered for a minute, "Want to talk over some tea?"

"Sure," I replied standing up. I wasn't surprised. We're trusting here in Minnesota and due to the extreme weather, it's common to invite people inside to talk. Who wants to talk standing around in the cold?

She led the way to the next house. "My name's Susan Yates. You're curious about the Sanders," she said opening her door with an electronic keypad. "I liked Beth but they weren't friendly neighbors."

"Anything you could tell me would help," I replied. I stepped out of my boots and followed her into a warm, homely kitchen with gleaming hardwood floors, and sat down.

"Why?" she asked heating up water for tea. "You said you were working for her attorney? Didn't she do it? I would have if he was my husband."

I paused to think, playing with the fur on the dog's head. He was a real lover and had his head in my lap soaking up all the scratching he could. I decided truth was my friend and I continued, "I'm

Chris and a friend of Beth's. I'm trying to make sense of all this. She doesn't remember what happened."

She nodded but didn't say anything. "Is this guy a Doberman?" I asked. He was tall and had the square head of a Doberman but his fur was not black and tan. He was an even mix of gray and white.

"No, he's a mutt I got from the shelter. I was looking for big and he got a bit bigger than I expected. I named him Baby."

"Rescue dogs are the best," I replied, grinning at the huge dog named Baby.

"Do you have a dog?"

"No, a spoiled cat. I wish I had a dog but I lost that argument several times."

She laughed. "I like having a dog because my husband is a doctor and he has really weird hours."

"So does mine. Did you know Beth?"

"A little. She spent a lot of time in the water in the summer and we talked a few times. I always wondered about her as she was skittish. My husband, Dan, told me to stay away as he thought she was probably in an abusive relationship and he wanted me to be safe."

"Why did he think that?"

"Shouting next door and her bruises mostly."

"Did she ever tell you she was scared or he was hurting her?"

"No."

I figured that was all I was going to get for now but the tea was quite good and I spent a few minutes just enjoying it and enjoying the big, soft, friendly dog who was now licking my hand.

"I think her husband was a scumbag," Susan blurted.

"Why?"

"You're another woman so you might get it," she said.

I nodded and kissed the top of the big dog's head. He pushed his head into my chest and sat on his own wagging tail. What a ham and affectionate friend for Susan.

"I got this monster of a dog because of him. I couldn't walk the streets next to my own home without feeling like he was watching. He tried to sweet talk me a couple of times when I was outside in the yard and it made my skin crawl. There was his wife a couple hundred feet away and he was sweet talking to me."

"What did he say?"

"Nothing that would hold up in a court or anything, just we should get together sometime, wink wink. Stuff like that. I knew what he meant and he knew I knew. I told him to back off, but that seemed to encourage him. I brought this guy home and you are the only one except my husband that he has liked."

"Smart move," I replied. "And this guy's good company on top of that."

"Yeah," she said smiling and snapped her fingers at him. He jumped up and ran to her almost knocking the cups off the table. "He eats his weight in expensive dog food and he is a bull in a china closet, but I am fond of him."

He licked her face and she giggled.

"I better get going," I said standing. "Can I come back and talk to you again?"

"Sure, we're friendly around here," she said still holding her dog. "I hope you find what you are looking for."

"Me too," I replied. I left wondering what I looking for exactly.

Outside it was dark and Josh was loitering around the corner.

"What did you learn?" he asked on the way to his car.

"Not much, Susan didn't like Ben because he was hitting on her." I felt like a failure—my first attempt at talking to the neighbors wasn't very productive, although I enjoyed talking to Susan.

"The fact Ben was hitting on the neighbor is good," Josh said. "Let's keep asking questions. Maybe he was having an affair. That opens up the door for lots of 'Other Dudes' who could have been mad enough to murder him in such a personal, brutal way."

He drove me to my car and asked me to tell him before I went to the courthouse so he could follow. Oh, yeah, that sounded fun.

"You want me to be some kind of bait?"

"No," he replied winging those eyebrows again. "You are not some kind of bait, you are a lamb to the slaughter."

If I had believed him, I would have been smarter and remembered my new key chain.

Chapter Nine

A Few Leads and a Following

Saturday morning found me still alone and grumpy. I like my husband's work ethic and I appreciate the good pay he earns but I honestly don't like waking up alone and I don't like my house so empty. A dog would be nice, but since that's not going to happen, those kids better find themselves pronto and come back home with bundles of grandbabies. And it better be soon.

I went out to my car just to go somewhere and the tire was flat. Why would an almost new tire suddenly go flat? I looked around and really wanted to run. Going back into the empty house while I was feeling this spooked was not an option. I marched over to Mindy's yellow house on the corner. Mindy answered the door in her bathrobe and slippers, holding a cup of coffee.

"Good morning, early bird," she groused and it didn't sound like a compliment.

"You got me into this!" I snapped back, "And I don't like feeling scared."

She was suddenly concerned and peered both directions out the door before pulling me inside.

"It's warmer now," she scolded, "but not warm enough to have a conversation on the doorstep." We don't talk to anyone on the doorstep in Minnesota, even delivery boys are asked in so the door can close while we are signing the receipts.

"My tire is flat," I grumbled.

"That is hardly a cause for concern," she argued. "An inconvenience maybe, but not a sign of evil-doing."

"Almost new," I snapped again. "And Josh wants to follow anyone who might be following me. I thought this was just going to be talking to people."

"Settle," Mindy said. "Have some coffee."

I glared at her.

"And some cinnamon buns that should be done in a few minutes," she added grabbing some frozen dough.

More bribery. It works, I never denied it.

While Mindy put together some almost-homemade cinnamon buns, I called the garage and had them come out to fix the tire.

Mindy made me eat the overly sweet and buttered buns with steaming coffee and lectured me on being paranoid while two tires were replaced and I handed over my credit card. Seems both front tires were flat with no obvious reason. Oh, yeah, I was being overly paranoid.

Still grumpy, I called Josh and asked him if I could talk to Beth before dark. He had an appointment and said 4:00 p.m. was the earliest. Not totally dark by then but pushing into the evening in Minnesota in the winter.

Going home to that empty house was not an option so I needed to think of something to do until 4:00 that involved people.

"Headed for the library," I announced standing up. "Anyone want to join me?"

I was surprised that both Mindy and her daughter April wanted to come. We decided to walk as we needed to work off the sugar and butter that makes cinnamon buns so good. It was only a mile to the regional library and stretching out into a brisk walk did feel good. I was pretty sure I spotted Guy in a running suit following but I was ignoring him and his ideas.

April needed to do some research on wolves for a class project and as soon as she was elbow deep in books. I headed for the internet.

"Why don't you do that at home?" Mindy asked me.

"The quiet is getting to me," I admitted. "Besides it feels safer here."

"Oh, yeah, the internet fairy can't find you here," she responded, grinning at me.

I looked up Ben's real estate company and read through a lot of interesting information on homes around us. He seemed to specialize in commercial property and according to his site he was buying and selling consistently. The phone number, email, and office address was on the front page but I wondered why they also had a "contact us" link. I clicked it and was told the page was unsecured. I shrugged, some people don't know how to build a website. I wanted to get the name of their "girl" so I picked up Mindy's cell phone and called the number for Ben's Real Deals from the homepage.

A sweet voice on a recording offered to take a message and I asked if someone could call me back and gave my cell number. I said I had a small piece of land just ripe for development and I wanted to know how much I could get for it. Not exactly a lie, the chunk of forest next to my house would make a nifty store location if someone wanted to kill all the trees.

Around noon we decided to stop researching and grab a bite. April and Mindy wanted to try a new little bistro on the corner so we wandered over there and had salads and amazing lattes with a hot cocoa for April.

By 3:30 I was headed for the courthouse for another little chat with Beth. Josh told me not to look for him but he was around. Wonderful. How could I be sarcastic with myself in my own head? I didn't know, but I needed to get a hold of my reactions. I needed to be patient and the picture of an interested third party.

I was let in to see Beth and I reminded her that this was a private conversation between her and her attorney's office and could not be recorded.

She was looking much better and actually laughed at me.

"I think it's for them, not you," I muttered, apologizing.

Her hands were no longer bandaged and she was rubbing them self-consciously. "These are going to scar, I think," she whispered.

I nodded and waited.

"What do you need to know?" she asked, finally.

"I'm looking for information to help your attorney. Any people you know who had an ax to grind with your husband, or you. Any information on his deals or friends would be helpful. Just talk to me."

"The cops already asked me that," she replied.

"Yup, but your attorney needs to know everything they know. Was your husband loyal to you?"

I asked that a bit point blank because I was tired of being patient.

"Probably not," she responded. So, I guess it wasn't too abrupt.

"You know that could give the cops some motive. Were you upset about it and could you have hurt him in anger?"

"Don't be crazy." Beth almost laughed as she said it. I was glad to see her coming back to this reality but surprised at her attitude. "I didn't care who or what he screwed. I tried to give up on him several times but then he wanted to try again. He was always saying if he could break through from his life we could be happy. Is he really dead?"

"I believe so. Why don't you?"

"I'm remembering things. I remember a lot of blood in the kitchen and a body covered in it. I did pick up a knife from the floor because it was there and then dropped it again because it was all bloody. I didn't go any closer and I didn't check to see if that person was dead. I ran. I ran right out onto the lake and almost across it before I got really disoriented."

"What do you think happened?"

"Someone was killed and it is somehow my fault. I'm always to blame when things go wrong. It's always my fault when a deal falls through. Everything was always my fault. Last month I was blamed for the cold weather. I like it here in lock up. No one hits me and if I do what I'm told, they leave me alone. Can I stay?"

"Is that why you are not out on bail?"

"I told my attorney I wouldn't pay any bail."

I decided to change tack. "Did you ever confront him or catch him?"

"No, I tried not to. He was very charming when on the prowl. Not so charming when mad."

"I get it. Some guys are only interested in the one that got away. It's the thrill of the chase they like."

She smiled a slow smile and it hit me that she could be very pretty, with that wide smile and those chocolate brown eyes.

"You look really pretty when you smile."

"Really?" she asked and actually blushed.

"Do you know any names or addresses of women he was seeing?"

"Well, he said Gabriela was sexy one night. And he said that Jolie liked it when he was rough. He seemed to think he was hurting me by telling me about them. I tried to care and pretended to be sad to make him happy."

"Was he fooled?"

"Sometimes," she smiled at me. "I don't know any Gabriela, but I think there was a Jolie Matthews. She called once and told me to tell him to leave her alone."

"Did you?"

"No, why stick the beast with a sharp thing?"

Why indeed.

"I'm pretty sure it was him that they found in the kitchen covered in blood. I don't think the medical examiner would be wrong about his identity," I said.

"Did they check his brother?"

"What?"

"His brother looks just like him and is meaner."

"What is his name?"

"Penn."

"Are you sure? That is a weird name."

"Weird family. When they were little, his mother always joked about Ben and Penn being the twin spawns of the Devil."

"Twins?" Now I was starting to get freaked out. "Are you sure?"

She shrugged. "Penn doesn't want people to know about him. I bet you can't find him. Their mom only filled out one birth certificate because they were identical twins."

"What?" I responded. "Why?"

"No idea," she said. "She had her own way of thinking. And it seemed to her that two were the same as one."

"Weird," I said. "Didn't the nurses object?"

"Nope, born at home, too cheap for a doctor or nurse."

"Wasn't it awkward for school?"

"No, they loved it. They took turns going to class and did all kinds of not-so-nice tricks on people."

"Easy to get a foolproof alibi that way," I reasoned.

"Yup, all the time. When they were both in a good mood and together they talked about how weird their mom was. They just said she had a loose screw or two but they appreciated having half the time each to do whatever they wanted. Not healthy in my mind, amazing they turned out as well as they did."

I was doubting either of them came into adulthood in one piece but I was not going to go down this rabbit hole with her.

"What if the dead person is your husband?"

"Then, I am even more scared of his brother. Is it evil to hope it was his brother?"

I was quiet. There didn't seem to be much hope for this trapped woman who seemed to think lock up was an improvement. And my mind wandered to that strange man who wanted to be called Guy and why he got me involved in this convoluted mess. I do have a soft spot for strays so maybe it's not his fault.

Then it occurred to me. "It must be your Ben that was dead. Wouldn't he be all over you spending his money on a good attorney if it wasn't him?"

She massaged her scarred hands and watched herself doing it. Finally, she looked up and said, "Maybe you're right." Then she shrugged. "No matter."

"No matter?" I blurted. "What do you want, Beth?"

She gave me a small, secretive smile and my stomach turned over and she looked down at her hands again.

"Beth," I said waiting until she looked up at me. "Did you kill your husband?"

"Don't think so," she replied quietly. "I can't say I remember exactly. But, I don't think so."

"What do you want your attorney to do?"

She shrugged. "Defend me," she whispered.

Well, fine and dandy is all I could think and yes, I was being sarcastic with myself again. Time to regroup, get home to a hot toddy and maybe a fire in the fireplace. Why was Beth back to whispering? Was she playing with a full deck? I just didn't know.

It was dusk when I headed to my car and I walked quickly. I was trying to convince myself that I was just skittish.

I heard the distant pounding of footsteps behind me and I struggled into my little Saturn quickly. I clicked the lock button before doing anything and exhaled when she started right up sounding all perky. Did I mention I love my little Saturn? I do. Then I looked around. It was that almost dark but bright time right after sunset. The wind stirred small swirls of snow across the road and if I didn't know better, I'd think it was peaceful. Why did I hear running footsteps but not see anyone?

Shaking my head at myself, I started down the empty city street. Two parked cars, and later an SUV pulled out a reasonable distance behind me. Was I being followed? I turned quickly onto a side street and the SUV went on past. Now I just felt silly.

It was a narrow side street and I turned around awkwardly and finally headed for the freeway. I went past an old, tan car that reminded me of Josh's car but it didn't move and I couldn't see anyone in it.

I merged onto the freeway and set the speed control. I love the way it will keep your speed even and you don't have to constantly be pushing the gas. I was tooling along feeling fine and relieved when I heard tires squealing. I looked in the rear-view mirror and there was Josh's car right on my tail. I thought he wanted to follow whomever was following me. What was going on?

I took a quick peek into my back seat with my heart pounding. Nope, empty. Why do we tell each other scary stories about bad guys hiding in the back seat?

The car that I thought was Josh was still driving close enough to hug my bumper so I swerved into the far lane. It barreled on past, ignoring me. Was I overreacting again to a rude driver?

A few miles later I saw the same car in the ditch, and Josh standing next to it. I slowed down and pulled over. When I unlocked the door, he jumped in, sliding really low in the back seat.

"Drive," was all he said.

I started the car moving before he even had his seat belt completely fastened. I was going to go to Hell for this I was sure.

"What's going on?" I demanded trying to look everywhere and still drive safely.

"Just drive," he responded, taking a deep breath.

I didn't say anything. Why so many men in my life with cryptic silence? Why wasn't Josh talking to me? Why did he try to live up to a negative stereotype? What was the deal with Guy, my stalker? Who was he, really? And why did he want me to save a woman who didn't want to be saved? Why was she better off now than before I got involved? What kind of convoluted murder was I sticking my customer service butt into? All these questions plagued me as I drove through traffic that was unusually heavy for this time of the day.

Suddenly, I had enough. I pulled over and braked quickly. He watched the cars going by and started to laugh.

"What?" I yelled totally frustrated.

"Smart move, you lost them," he said. "Totally unexpected move."

"What? Why is your car in the ditch?"

"They made me and were chasing me, actually shot at me a couple of times."

I stared at him and I think my mouth dropped open.

"Drove me off the road but not before I warned you," he said warmly. "Good job."

"What warn—I thought you were driving crazy!"

He smiled at me, all pretense of acting the big bad PI gone. "Good job anyway," he said. "You were right. Someone is very unhappy we are helping Beth."

"What now?" I asked. "I'm not really an action hero type. I'm into customer service and building team spirit and stuff."

"If that includes getting people to talk to you," he said leaning back in the seat. "This is a good career move for you."

"Yeah, right," I replied, pulling back into traffic. "My super power is talking."

"Take this next exit," he said. "Getting people to talk," he corrected.

I turned on the exit; it was a bit slippery and it was a road I had never driven before. It was also not a neighborhood I'd walk in without a big dog.

"Next left," was Josh's only comment.

I pulled into a strip mall parking lot and he jumped out.

"Wait here," he ordered and disappeared into a shabby office building.

I locked the doors and tried to see all around my parked car at the same time. It was exhausting.

Josh appeared at the passenger window without me seeing him come back out. Great! Another failure to prove this was not the direction my life should be taking.

He rapped on the window and I jumped and clicked the lock. He slid his long body into the tiny seat and grinned at me. It occurred to me that he was enjoying this.

"Where to, boss?" I managed to say.

"Back to my car, my phone broke when I went in the ditch and I need to call a tow."

I dug with one hand into my purse and tried to hand him my phone, as I drove out of the parking lot and turned onto the access road.

"I didn't want to sit around and wait for them to double back. By leaving and coming back it's less likely they will be waiting," he answered, smiling. "And I picked up my spare."

Instead of being smart and catching that "less likely" I glommed onto the existence of an extra phone.

"You feel the need to have multiple cell phones?" I asked. "Why?"

"Only one, the one that broke is connected to the PI firm," he replied. "Sometimes it's nice to use a number the person receiving the call can't identify quickly. Even 'burner' phones can be traced eventually by the cops but a skip won't know."

"You do skip tracing?"

"No, not usually. I do background and secondary investigation for criminal attorneys. I used to be a cop but I like a looser management structure."

"You are sort-of scaring me right now," I said. "Why looser?"

Again that grin and the eyebrows going up and down.

"I need to go home," I said primly.

At that he laughed heartily, leaning back in the seat to give his guffaws all the air they needed.

"You are one-of-a-kind," was all he managed to say.

I didn't understand and frankly I was losing interest in understanding. I just wanted to be safe and the people I like to be safe. I drove silently.

"I called the tow truck at the office," he said finally. "You can just drop me."

"I don't think I would feel good about that," I returned, my Minnesota guilt in full regalia. "Young fellow like you, alone and scared at the side of the road."

This time when he laughed I joined him.

But when we got to his car it was very dark and I was having second thoughts. This felt real, and dangerous. I stopped right behind the spot his car left the road and left the car running.

"Now what?"

"Wait for the tow truck with me if you want."

It wasn't a long wait and it pulled up in front of my car.

"Thanks," he mumbled as he jumped out of the car. He walked over to the driver's side of the tow truck talking to the driver.

I saw movement in the gully with the car. I could make out a person, or two people creeping up the slope. Do I drive off and save myself? Smartest move but I couldn't do that. I just couldn't.

"Josh!" I yelled, half jumping out the car and throwing the only thing in my hand at the moving shadows. It was my phone. Okay, stupid, was all I could think as I dropped back into my seat and slid as low as I could. The phone hit a shadow and it flashed, showing two rather big men.

Josh moved quickly and came around to my car, while the tow truck decided to leave.

"Drive fool!" he yelled diving into the back seat.

I did and I heard muffled yelling behind us. Josh used his phone to call the police. We were down to one phone now.

"I just rescued you, you big, long joke," I yelled full of adrenaline. "And you called me a fool!"

"Couldn't you think of anything to throw besides your phone?"

"Not at the moment," I muttered, annoyed. We only drove a few miles and waited for the cops. I really wished I had remembered that canister of mace.

As the two had disappeared by the time the police came, there was not much to do besides get a new tow truck and get home.

I wimped out and asked for help finding my phone in the ditch and if someone would follow me home. Josh told me to put the cost of replacing it on my bill and I stared at him. "I have to make out an invoice?" I managed to grind out.

"Yup," he chirped back. He was in a very good mood. In my opinion, being chased is not a fun thing but I appeared to be in the minority here. I glared at the cops laughing and joking with Josh until I realized they didn't notice.

At home, all the lights were on and a movie marathon was on my other half's mind. He did take a minute to hug me and tell me I was amazing. It bothered me a little he wasn't worried about me, but it was nice he believed in me. The hug was warm and the movie was not a bad idea as the screen of flashing lights can make you forget the real boogie monster out there in the dark.

Chapter Ten

Lady Friend and Beanbags

Sunday morning was lazy and we made breakfast together and talked. Kristoff did not laugh at me for being crazy enough to throw a phone. He laughed because he thought it was a good idea. Turns out he was hit by a thrown phone and it hurt and flashed like mine did. The phone he was hit with wasn't even thrown on purpose, one of those weird accidents that can happen at work.

He talked me into checking out the phone. It was dead when I found it in the ditch but I plugged it in overnight anyway and didn't think about it again.

It had a charge. I checked the pictures and I had a really nice picture of a coat and the snow-covered ground. Well, I didn't expect more.

"Eureka!" I exclaimed. "Now we know it was someone in a brown coat."

"You know it was someone besides Beth," he replied soberly. "Maybe this isn't such a good idea, it seems a little dangerous."

"I agree," I mumbled. "But I can't seem to stop."

"What did you have planned today?" he asked with his evil grin.

I couldn't think of a thing as my brain turned off and I went over to his side of the breakfast nook to give him a kiss.

Later we showered and went to the shopping center to sign up for a martial arts class and see if we could find anything I could carry that might be more appropriate to throw. I seem to have a tendency to throw things so maybe some heavy bean bags would be more cost efficient than a phone or bottle of Merlot. I know, bean bags? But, I don't want anything resembling a weapon going to work and I do like to throw things. We then went to a game center where they have batting cages and places to practice pitching. I had fun practicing my aim, which was better than I expected.

We drove home in good spirits but our laughter died when we drove up to the house to see the garage covered in ugly, red paint messages. Several of the suggestions were anatomically impossible and several were just not true. But they were definitely threatening and hateful.

"Too cold to paint," was his only comment.

"Well—" I started to say but swallowed it. I wasn't going to be forced to start swearing and I guess

I wasn't going to be forced to do anything, even stop asking questions.

I looked at him and blurted, "You work so many hours! I'm alone in this house too much!"

He didn't have an answer. What could he do? Quit his job that paid most of the bills?

"I want a dog!" I continued. I knew he didn't want a dog. He has allergy problems. But, enough was enough. "I hate to be scared," I finished almost whimpering.

Kristoff turned the car around and headed to the animal shelter. I sat in the car in shocked silence. After all the disagreements we had on pet ownership, he was taking the lead in getting me a dog.

We got there at 5:30 and the sign said they closed at 6:00 p.m. Could we find an animal that would fit into our lives and be able to protect us in under thirty minutes?

Turns out we could. I told the lady I wanted a dog for protection, but my husband had allergies. I didn't mind an older dog but asked what could be done about the allergies. She said regular baths and brushing would greatly reduce allergy problems. Well then, I wanted a dog that likes baths.

She laughed a pleasant, low rumble, and we walked into the back. I wanted to take them all home, from the cute little squawk-boxes to the huge ponies in dog suits.

A funny-looking shepherd-collie mix was sitting in her water bowl and I took that as a sign she wouldn't hate baths.

"I bet that one won't mind baths," I said pointing. The attendant opened the door and the big girl started shaking.

"Was she abused?" I asked.

"You never know for sure here," the lady replied. "But I don't think so, she's a sweet one and think she's just excited."

"What's her name?"

"Lady."

"Really? So unoriginal!"

She shrugged.

"Hey there, friend," I said to the shaking dog who wagged her tail twice, splashing water all over the pen.

"Wanna come home with me and protect me?"

She stood up and wagged her tail again and still shaking all over.

"Come," I said, putting out both hands and she came to me in one long lope.

I hunkered down and wrapped my arms around her big shoulders and hugged her while she tried to lick the back of my neck.

"I think you've had some serious training," I whispered to her and she wagged her tail so hard her whole body wagged.

"This one," I said. "But her name is Friend. So, sweetie," I said to her. "Do you like chasing bean bags?

She licked my face thoroughly and I ended up sitting on the floor laughing.

My husband just watched from a distance. His eyes were turning red, but he was smiling.

"She is a mess," he said. "Good thing we came in your car."

"Yup, my Saturn will never smell the same," I agreed between face licks.

We had to pay a fee for her shots and a vet exam that the shelter requires. Then we trouped to the car with a crude rope lead and a happy dog as they locked up behind us.

"Stop at the pet store for supplies?"

I just nodded, my throat too thick to speak. Lady Friend just laid out on the back seat as if she had always been ours.

We went to one of those pet stores that allow you to bring your pet in the store. I had her sniff all the dog beds until there was one she kept going back to. I didn't let her pick the dog food. We went with organic and healthy and told her she would like it. She looked at me like she understood and started sniffing the treat shelf.

"Okay, treats you pick."

To suit her new name, we picked out a pink collar and lead. She didn't seem to have an opinion on that. I picked up a purple and pink dog blanket for the back seat of my car that both Lady Friend and my husband ignored.

Finally, I asked a staff member for advice on dog shampoos. I needed one I could use regularly that would help my poor, abused husband and wouldn't hurt her with frequent use.

We left after the second, expensive stop with a trunkful of supplies. I laid out the blanket on the back seat and put her new collar on before letting her in the car. She sat very quietly for this and gave my face a quick lick before jumping in and checking out her new travel bed.

"She is very well mannered," my husband commented closing the trunk. "I think she will know how to protect you."

"I do too," I said. "But now, I just want to protect her."

We made one last stop at the pharmacy for eye drops and allergy pills. Lady Friend and I waited in the car having a long conversation. I was the only talking with words, but I already believed she understood me and answered with licks or tail wagging. She also had a wide range of face expressions and she used her eyebrows to show attention.

The garage didn't look so bad in the dark when we got home. "Too cold to paint for real," I said, "but we could spray on some red paint, so it just looks all red."

"If you want, it will have to be redone in the summer, but do the front door also, I've always wanted a red front door."

"Anything for you!" I replied. "I can't tell you how much this means!"

"You don't have to," he said smiling. "I saw you sitting on the floor and laughing."

"Hey, Lady Friend," I said turning around to face the back seat. She sat up her attention totally on my face.

"Want to have a bathroom break and check out the yard?" She responded with a single swipe of her tail.

"I don't think I need a lead for her," I said getting out and opening the door. "I believe she's well-trained."

"Don't lose her," he responded opening the trunk and shouldering the huge bag of dog food. "Already cost us an arm and a leg."

"Ha," I said opening the door and slapping my leg. She jumped out and stood next to me leaning into my leg.

"This is now your yard," I told her. "Let's walk around it so you know the area."

We walked all the way around the yard with her staying close enough to touch the entire time.

On the way to the backyard she did her business and we went in the rear.

My husband met us on the stairs with his allergy pills in one hand and the shampoo in the other hand.

"You better like baths," I laughed grabbing the shampoo and headed for the bathroom. She followed, and we had a very messy, very wet time. Okay, she didn't hate the bath and she liked the attention. But she made sure that I got just as wet as she did. My spoiled cat, Pudding, ignored the whole thing and hid.

Drying involved a thorough brushing and I set up her bed in a warm spot near the heat register and the front door. "This is your post, sweetie," I said through a face lick.

I then went down to the laundry and stripped, putting all my wet, fur-covered clothes directly into the washing machine.

I turned around and there was my husband grinning like a loon. "Wet and naked," he said. "Just the way I like my women."

"Ha," I replied. But it was a little bit before I made it upstairs in my warm robe to feed the new addition to my family.

Chapter Eleven

Real Deals is Real

Monday morning started quietly. It was cold and grey outside but not frigid nor stormy. I was pretty sure I saw my personal stalker standing at the edge of the road but I was busy ignoring him.

Gretchen met me at the door and told me that she went to Walmart to see Gabriela.

"Why?" was my reaction.

"I still think she hurt Frank," Gretchen responded. "Don't you want to sniff around?"

"No," I responded.

Gretchen shrugged. "Well," she said. "I'm watching her and her wicked ways."

Oh, my.

"Gretchen, you have three little kids," I said reasonably. "You don't have time for this. And it's not safe."

"My uncle said the same thing," she responded with a laugh. "Don't worry so. I'll tell you if I find anything."

"Don't find anything, we don't have time for you to find anything," I responded. "We're testing the new scheduling system today."

"I know, it's not working."

A few hours later I was drowning in emails about the new scheduling system and what we needed to do to get it working. My cell phone rang and it was Ben's Real Deals. The same sweet voice as the recording asked me for an appointment to see the land for listing.

I had no intention of killing my wonderful trees to make a few bucks so a store could go in right next to me. But, I did want to talk to someone from Ben Sander's office so I made an appointment for that evening after work.

"Can I come to the office first?" I asked, thinking this might be my only chance to meet "The Girl."

"I've heard good things about Ben," I said, suddenly inspired. "I want to deal with him exclusively."

"Oh, dear," the sweet voice responded. "He's not available. His partner and I would love to get things started at least."

This was interesting. First, were they not telling clients that Ben was gone? And second, maybe the girl was more than an underpaid, unnamed office perk. This was a development.

My next move was to call Josh and tell him where I was going. He approved but wanted to come. I refused, which was not the smartest move of the day. But I was thinking that it would be harder to get information if he was around looking tough.

When it was time to clock out for the day, I opened several new tickets requesting help from the IT department with our scheduling system and headed out to Real Deals.

The office was all chrome and modern efficiency. Clean lines and a feeling that bordered on sterile. An elegant, well-groomed beauty was sitting at the front desk. She smiled with her lips and mouth, but her eyes seemed dull and didn't focus on my face. They focused on the picture on the far wall. I stepped between her and the picture and her green eyes focused on me and seemed surprised. I almost laughed, and she smiled in appreciation. She had long, silver blonde hair and was twenty-five years old tops. Her green eyes were well defined with artfully applied makeup.

"I'm Chris," I said helpfully, holding out my hand. She pulled out a hand with a French manicure and shook my hand. Well, more she slid her limp hand over mine and quickly pulled it back.

"My name is Naomi," she replied. "Naomi Pyle and I'm glad to meet you."

No, she would be glad to buy my nice piece of land and pay someone to bulldoze the trees. I wondered which partner she was sleeping with and shook my head a little to dislodge the admitted prejudice. Just because she was beautiful and well-groomed did not mean she was someone's trollop and just because she wanted to see my lot for possible business use did not mean she was a tree killer. But, I did have a name for their "girl" and I had to admit to myself she was probably not an innocent bystander or pawn. I was suddenly reminded of an old saying; when two witches meet, if they don't both laugh, one of them isn't a witch.

"Well hello there!" came a booming voice from the office to the left.

"It's your four o'clock," Naomi said.

"Here you are!" a compact man in an expensive suit gushed coming out of his office. He clasped my hand in a strong shake that bordered on too long and too hard.

"Andy?" I asked.

"Yes! You got it!" he responded. I felt positive that this man would be an excellent salesman and if I wanted to sell my land he would get the best price.

"What about Ben Sanders?" I asked. "It's his reputation for getting a great price that brought me here."

"Sorry," he whispered conspiratorially. "Second honeymoon."

"Really? What about his brother?"

I heard Naomi take a deep breath and looked at her. She had become a very pale version of herself. And within a few seconds it passed, and she looked as cool and calm as a tiger on a hunt.

Andy's face was just a studied confused frown. "Don't think he has a brother," he said pensively. Was Andy just a much better liar or was Naomi the only one who could confirm Beth's assertion that there was a brother? If Naomi's face was any indication, the brother was scary.

I saw my stalker standing outside the window on the sidewalk. As he seemed to show up when there was danger, I decided I didn't want to ask any more questions.

"I'll wait to see Ben if you don't mind," I hedged.

"Well now—" Andy started.

"It might be some time," Naomi blurted.

Andy gave her a look and she sat down and started typing. "Let me have a look at your plot and see if I can find a number that will change your mind," he practically purred.

"Fine," I replied, and wrote down the address. "Meet you there."

I walked out quickly and scrambled into my little Saturn. I drove to my place, watching him follow. I made a quick call to Josh telling him where we were and inviting his voicemail to join me.

I parked in my driveway and fetched Lady Friend. We walked to the far edge of the mowed lawn. Here were tall trees and tangled undergrowth. I loved having a buffer of woods between me and the neighbors. The squirrels were chattering and dropped some bits of wood on us.

"Woof," she barked once and looked at them and then back at me pointedly.

"Does no good to chase squirrels," I hunched down and ruffled her neck, getting her attention on me and not the loud, aggressive squirrels.

Andy walked up smiling. "Now this is a picture," he commented. "Lady and her dog."

"Dog's name is Lady Friend," I replied letting go of her neck and standing. She looked at Andy and growled low without moving or even twitching.

He took one step back then looked at the trees. "Well, it would have to be cleared of all this deadwood before putting it on the market."

I put my hand on Lady Friend's head and cocked my head. "What could you get for it as is?"

"Is it a full lot?"

"Lot and a half, it goes all the way back."

"Nice, I'll put together some numbers and what you could get cleared."

I couldn't wait to have him off my land and away from me so I just nodded. "Send it to my email."

"Oh, I'll deliver it in person, so I can answer any questions right away."

I nodded and backed away. I so wished Josh was around. "Call first," I said and turned around heading for my house. Why was I so nervous? Just because my stalker showed up outside his office didn't mean Andy was dangerous, did it? Just because I knew he was lying to me about Ben was no reason to assume the worst, or was it? I didn't understand completely but I also didn't want to find out. I realized I must trust that quiet man in the shadows at least a little.

"Hold on, little lady," Andy grabbed my arm and Lady Friend growled.

He dropped my arm as the fur on top of my rather large dog's neck stood up and she placed herself between us.

"I don't get the feeling you trust me," he said. "Why am I feeling that way?"

"Because I don't," I snapped. "Second honeymoon, my foot! My friend Beth is locked up and Ben is dead! Why would you lie to me about that?"

"Bad for business," he shrugged. "Do you really want a quote on this prime piece of land?"

"Couldn't hurt," I returned. "Maybe I'll move somewhere with no neighbors."

"That's the spirit!" he said smiling.

Okay, now my mind was reeling. "What is your relationship with Naomi?" I asked quietly.

He went still. "Why are you asking about that?"

I shrugged.

"Why is everyone asking me about my relationship with her? No one's business!"

"So, you are having an affair?"

"Don't go there!"

"Was Ben also having an affair with her?"

"Ben was an asshole and I made sure she was safe from him."

"You killed Ben?"

"No, you idiot!" he yelled, and Lady Friend started barking wildly. She pushed against me and wouldn't stop barking.

"Control that dog!" he stuttered, backing away.

I stood with my hand on her as he backed all the way to his car, got in and drove off. I didn't believe Andy was an innocent bystander with all his lies and his protective attitude towards Naomi, who I was sure knew about the brother. Andy was involved, I just didn't know how much.

"Good girl," was all I said.

Chapter Twelve

Bad Aim, Wrong Target

I gave my wonderful dog a few treats and started boiling some water for tea. I took out the brandy and waited for the water. A stronger cup of tea was on my mind. The doorbell rang, and I wasn't even sure I was going to answer. Lady Friend whined by the door so I went over. It was Josh and I let him in.

"Want a cup of tea?" I asked him as he shed layers of coat and sweater.

"Sure, but could you please stop scaring me?" he asked, his rangy legs sticking out under my table.

"I think we have more to pile on the Some Other Dude Defense," was my response.

I explained to him the responses of Andy and how he said he protected Naomi from Ben.

"All good information," Josh agreed. "You are well worth your pay."

"You aren't paying me!" I retorted with a huff.

"Maybe we should," he laughed. "This is pretty good tea."

"Go home to your new wife!" I replied. "Take some with you."

"Thought you would never offer, but please let me be around when you do this kind of questioning with possible suspects."

I nodded agreement and walked him to the door.

"Lock it," he commented, patting the side of the door.

I was mixing hamburger with eggs, oatmeal and chunks of sweet peppers and onions to make meatloaf when I heard the garage door open. Oh, good. I smiled. My geek husband was coming home in time for supper.

I added salt and pepper and got out the baking dish and still nobody kissing me over the stove.

"Sweetie?" I called.

Lady Friend growled, and I walked to the stairs with my ceramic baking dish.

"Lady Friend," I whispered. "Who is it?"

She erupted in barking and tore down the stairs. The knob to the door into the garage was turning slowly.

My heart was in my chest as I waited with a buttered casserole dish in my hands.

It opened slowly, and I threw the dish as hard as I could. It missed my husband by a few inches and broke on the door frame.

His eyes got huge behind his oversized glasses and he ducked after the fact. Lucky I was a bad aim.

Before he could yell at me, I yelled at him, "What are you doing scaring me?"

He shrugged his shoulders, his eyes still huge. "I guess I didn't think coming home through the garage would scare you. Should I call first?"

"No, don't be dense!" I shouted. I probably shouldn't have shouted, but I was feeling shaky and very upset I almost hurt someone I love.

"Listen here," he countered in a fake accent. "If you are going to attack and insult me the least you can do is give me a smooch."

I snickered and came down the stairs for a very brief, hard hug. What if I had hurt him? Why did Lady Friend act that way?

"Lady Friend," I said to the big dog who was acting like she wasn't a part of this. She wagged her tail. "Why did you bark at a friend?"

She wagged her tail once.

"I don't think she's going to be able to explain herself," he said. "No treats for her."

She whined and sat down giving him the begging head tilt.

"Really?" I laughed. "You are so easily bought!"

She stayed sitting but wagged her tail and offered a paw.

"Okay, peace, it is," he replied taking the paw and shaking it.

I swept the broken dish up and took the full dustpan outside to dump directly into the trash bin. It was dark outside the garage even with the lights we had just installed. It was too cold to stop and wonder why it was so quiet, but then I saw someone or something move just a few feet off the driveway into the yard.

"Hello?" I ventured. And then there was nothing, just shifting shadows. I backed into the garage, watching the darkness and seeing nothing. A yelp made me jump forwards and almost fall as Lady Friend pushed by me and ran into the snowy yard.

I looked towards the house and my husband was standing in the open door. He shrugged. "Dog wanted out," he said.

"Come on back here," I yelled, and she bounded back to lick my face.

"What did you find?" I inquired as if she could answer. But she had no answer for me and just wanted to go in. It was time for her bath anyway.

"Better locks," I muttered going in with my dog. "We need better locks."

Chapter Thirteen

Doughnuts and Magic

Morning found me still tired and grumpy. The alarm was very insistent in the dark. I didn't want to get up. Outside was just as gloomy as me with a cold, grey darkness that promised a storm before long.

"A storm," I muttered to myself as I drove to work. "Just what we need." Okay, so now I was being grumpy talking to myself. That would not do. How can I sell myself as a customer service specialist supervising a customer service department if I was grumpy with myself? This had to stop and stop now. I pulled over by the frozen lake to give myself a serious talking-to.

The lake was forlorn and cold without even a stiff breeze to keep it company. The ice houses looked like a frozen, deserted city in another world. They were a hodgepodge of sheds clustered together. A few had paint and finishing touches but most of them were raw wood held together by a few well-placed nails or screws. I decided a firm talking-to could wait. What I really needed was sugar and caffeine, and lots of it.

I arrived at work with doughnuts and coffee, enough for an army. All the smiles and appreciation made it well worth the cost and it put the bounce back into my step.

"Can we have lunch?" Gretchen mumbled through her mouth full of doughnut.

"You're choking on a doughnut and thinking about lunch?" I laughed.

She nodded her chocolate brown eyes very serious.

"Just you and me, kid," I said.

Later in the day, we actually left the building and went to a sit-down cafe not far from work. Gretchen was serious and pensive on the way over.

Finally, sitting down, I blurted, "Spit it out. What is going on?" Have I mentioned my very effective subtle approach to management? Okay, I've been told I don't have a subtle bone in my body. How does direct and customer service mix? Very well actually.

"I actually talked to Gabriela," she said, checking out the menu while a waitress headed our way. We would not have a lot of time away from the job and we needed to order quickly. "I think a huge burger would be in order today."

"With fries?" I asked smiling.

"Of course," she said quickly, "and an ice tea."

"Me too," I said to the waitress and waited for her to leave.

"So, why did you decide to talk to Gabriela? We both know she threatened and scared people."

"Yeah, but why?"

"I don't know and frankly I don't want to know."

"Well, I did," Gretchen snapped.

"Why are you angry with me?" I asked. This seemed to be getting into a sensitive area and I was feeling like I was standing on shifting ground.

"Not you exactly," Gretchen replied quietly. "But so many people judge and make decisions without all the facts."

"This is true," I said, smiling at the waitress returning with our huge glasses of iced tea. I waited for her to continue as she obviously had a lot to unload. And honestly this is what I am good at. People talk to me.

"She's a mess," Gretchen added adding copious amounts of sugar to her tea.

I nodded, sipping my tea. It would have been better with a little brandy or a good French Liqueur, but this was only lunch and I couldn't go back to work with alcohol in my system. Too bad. Maybe later

I would be able to curl up with Lady Friend and hot tea with brandy. The thought made me smile.

"I feel bad for her," Gretchen muttered almost apologetically. "I know she was disruptive when she worked with us."

I didn't know how to answer that. Gabriela freaked out my trainer by telling the training class she was afraid of her son because she killed his father and was concerned it affected him. She then proceeded to seduce a vulnerable older veteran and try to get him into trouble with me. She might have frightened him badly enough that he fell down a flight of stairs in the dark, breaking his leg. None of this caused any problems for her but I was glad she missed enough days that I could terminate her for attendance per our regulations. She was not a positive member of our team.

Instead of answering, I just nodded and smiled at the waitress who was coming over with huge platters of thick hamburgers and all the fixings.

"Say something," Gretchen demanded.

"What do you want me to say? I don't trust her, she is a negative person who leaves bodies in her wake."

"Funny," Gretchen returned, back to a little snappish.

"Not trying to be funny," I responded, trying to understand her mood. "I found her a negative force and not terribly customer-service oriented. I am not sorry she is gone but I did nothing to force the issue as that would be against our HR policies."

Gretchen just looked at me and I was reminded that I may not be understanding where she was coming from.

"I'm sure she is a mess," I admitted. "She said she killed her baby daddy because he was violent and that is very possible. We know she was never convicted for a murder she told us she did and we don't know why. I was told there was insufficient evidence and no murder weapon by Frank after he reported to the police that she threatened him and told him she had used it. But that has to be treated like an unsubstantiated rumor."

Gretchen continued to just look at me.

"Okay," I admitted. "That would be the definition of a mess."

Gretchen smiled and took a huge bite of her burger.

I was feeling very unsatisfied by this conversation but decided to let it stew a minute and sample my burger. It was very juicy, and the fries were crunchy on the outside and soft in the middle.

There was some time where the only sounds were crunching and chewing and few murmurs of enjoyment.

Finally, when there was nothing on her plate but two French fry ends and smear of ketchup, Gretchen looked up at me. "We went for coffee and talked for a long time. She is sure all men are out to hurt her and that the magic is fading in her life."

"Magic?"

"Yeah, that had me stumped too. It seems she dabbles a little in magic and thinks that she's been cut off since working for you."

"Hummm," was all that wanted to come out of my mouth. I scratched my head. "So, she thinks I took away her magic?"

"Well, no, she didn't say that."

I frowned at Gretchen. "What exactly did she say?"

I felt like I was twitching under my skin and I wanted to explode. I did not, I do not, I would have no idea how to cut off someone's magic. I don't even think I would know what that was unless it jumped up and bit me. And I still would probably not recognize it.

"And don't forget Frank ended up dead," I added for good measure.

"It was ruled natural causes," she replied.

"Yes, it was. I never understood how a throat could explode and they call it natural causes."

"Maybe he had untreated cancer or something," she replied.

"Maybe," I agreed. There was no point in disagreeing as nothing about Frank dying made sense to me, other than the fact he had the worst luck I ever experienced. And I have seen a lot of bad luck stories working with entry level employees in a call center.

"Did she happen to mention dating a guy named Ben?" I asked casually. There are not that many Gabrielas around, it was possible.

"No, why?" she asked.

I shrugged. It was a long shot. Maybe I needed something from Walmart.

Chapter Fourteen

Privacy Laws and Flowers

After talking to Gretchen, I could not focus back on the broken scheduling program. I had more disgruntled customers escalated to me and the only solution I could see was to fix the scheduling program, so we would be better at getting to the place on time.

An escalated caller put a bug in my ear by accusing me of knowing where she went and with whom from my database. It made me wonder what I could find about Penn or Ben in my system. But it was against privacy laws to look at a person's account without their permission. I explained that in detail and she calmed down and told me that she didn't call, and I was not to log her calling. I decided not to explain to her I had no choice, it logged automatically. I was pretty sure a headache was lurking in the back of my brain, so I went for more coffee.

On my desk when I returned was a large assortment of flowers. White lilies and bright red poppies mixed in with three beautiful orchids. One of the orchids was pure white, towering over the other flowers. The other two orchids matched the red of the poppies and mixed into the center of the arrangement. The vase was an hourglass shape and a pale blue, like ice. It was as an elegant vase, like the flowers. I fully expected a note from my sweet guy, but the note was in bold old-fashioned cursive, not his style at all. It said, "Be careful."

Gretchen walked by with a grin and a laugh in her dark eyes.

"I didn't expect you to have a secret admirer." she said.

"Not my husband," I muttered more to myself than her. But she laughed.

Flowers from my stalker who seemed to always be close. And in a secure building. I shivered. At least they were pretty and smelled of cinnamon, spice and ozone. Like a wild storm coming.

I was so tempted to do some research on back calls and check out a Beth Sanders, Ben Sanders, or Penn Sanders phone records. So illegal. So, tempting.

I ate a spare chocolate bar to distract myself.

Didn't work.

I stared at the juxtaposition of lilies and poppies and wondered where someone could get poppies this time of year. But that allowed my brain to wander and I went over what I had just said to the angry caller again. It's against privacy laws to look without permission. Beth could give me permission.

I grabbed my laptop and told my supervisor I was leaving early. She just nodded.

The courthouse was deserted and quiet. I guess late afternoon on a Thursday is not their busy time. My footsteps echoed, and the ceiling seemed higher than the other days I visited.

Maybe I was losing it. I asked if I could see Beth, and agreed it was not scheduled. The greying security guard was friendly and set it up.

Beth seemed surprised to see me and she was looking healthy. Her eyes were still a little sunken, but her skin was glowing from a recent shower.

"Strange time to visit," she said after my odd introduction declaring this was a private conversation between her attorney's office and her.

I nodded my agreement. "What kind of phones did you and Ben use?"

"All three of us had iPhones."

"Did you use Find my Phone?"

"I think so, why?"

I booted up my laptop and signed in. I opened it to the cloud and twisted it to Beth.

"Sign in," I said.

She frowned at me but did.

"Okay, look," I said. "Three little green dots, are they all iPhones?"

"Yeah, me, and Ben and Penn, why?"

"Well two are here in the city and one is in Clearwater."

"Oh," she whispered.

"Ben's should have been turned off by now," I said thinking.

"No, I had mine and Ben's in my purse. The guards have them."

"The third?"

"Penn's," she said very quietly.

"Why Clearwater?"

She looked away from me.

"Beth," I said quietly.

She looked back and then lowered her gaze to the table.

"Cabin," she whispered.

"Give me the address," I demanded.

She shrugged and typed it onto a sticky on my laptop.

It was full dark, and the wind whipped my scarf on the way to my car. I had my keys with my pepper spray in my hand. I did not want to be interrupted I wanted to get home.

My stalker was standing close to the car but in the shadows. Did I want to confront him? Why did he send flowers to my work? Even more weird, how did he send flowers to my work and get them delivered behind security doors? The United States' Department of Justice is one of our clients for Pete's sake, our security was tight. Why—and again how—would he be able to effect Gabriele's magic? Did I even believe she had magic to be taken away? Why was he hanging around? There were certainly more interesting people than me to follow, right?

No, I really didn't want to confront him, not really. I stormed to the car daring anyone to come between me and something for this headache.

Chapter Fifteen

Scared Dog

I expected to relax and detox when I lumbered home with a massive headache and a yen for fried foods. Why does a headache make me want a fried egg with bacon? I have no logical reason for it.

Instead of peace when I turned into my driveway and got out of the car, I could hear my sweet-tempered dog howling and maybe actually throwing herself at the door. I opened it quickly and she thundered out, almost knocking me down. She went directly to the spot on the side of the driveway where I thought I saw movement last night, sat herself down and turned her pretty face to the cold winter sky and howled.

I looked around quickly wondering how long before the neighbors would be lodging formal complaints. "Sweetie," I crooned going to her and hugging her until she stopped and started licking me. "What's wrong?"

She sniffed and licked and checked me over but was unable to speak her fears. She was terrified, that much I could tell. "Oh, baby, what happened?" I crooned, starting back towards the house. She would have nothing to do with that until we walked all the way around the yard and sniffed all the corners. She herded me, pushing against my legs and circling me the entire time. I started laughing and my headache seemed to be receding.

"You are definitely part shepherd," I whispered to her. She wagged her tail once in response to my voice but was not distracted. We checked the perimeter. No other explanation for it. And then she was ready to go in and act like a normal dog.

"Be calm, Lady Friend," I murmured. "Food for both of us then a bath for each of us." She sat down and offered her paw.

I threw together a small salad and started grilling a hamburger for myself. At the last minute I threw a second one on for her. She needed a treat.

I watched the dark windows and wondered what happened out there today when I was gone. I just couldn't see the reasonable huge dog hanging out close to me all evening being neurotic or crazy.

Before our baths I called Mindy and asked her if she saw anything in my yard today. Mindy said she was in court all day and was not watching my yard. I was almost insulted but then she offered to come over for a cup of tea. I agreed to the tea—brandy was not a good idea with the remnants of a headache still lurking in the back of my head. I then called Josh's voicemail and asked him how much it would cost to put in a surveillance camera in my yard.

After tea, Mindy offered to let Lady Friend visit while I was at work as she was just doing paperwork at home Friday. That worked for tomorrow, but I could not afford to put her in pet daycare long-term. I took a very long bath after giving Lady Friend hers and tried not to be frustrated. It seemed every solution to a problem came with new problems.

I fell asleep quickly and only slightly noticed when the love of my life snuggled into bed around 3:00 a.m., trying not to wake me.

Chapter Sixteen

Yelling into the Wind

Friday morning started with a bang. It was a sharp crack that sounded like thunder or a car backfiring. Lady Friend jumped up on the bed between us and put her head down and whined once.

Kristoff sat up and looked around, but it was dark and there was nothing to see.

"S'okay, baby," I murmured, stroking the dog.

"Was that inside or out?" he asked.

"Outside, I'm pretty sure," I whispered.

"Why are you whispering?"

"Cause it's so quiet."

He laughed. "And what is the big, bad watch dog doing on the bed?"

"She's scared."

"Wonderful."

I got up and started off to the kitchen to put on some coffee and that's when we heard sirens.

I looked out the back window and down on the road there was smoke coming from the power pole. Two fire engines were pulling up below it.

"I never saw a transformer do that," I said.

"I have," my husband commented over my shoulder.

"I'll be late tonight," I reminded him. "I promised Josh we could 'do the neighborhood' tonight."

'Remember your pepper spray," he countered, "Nice neighborhoods can be deceptively dangerous."

He had a point.

The drive to work was quiet but the clouds were building. A storm was coming and would probably be here before tomorrow.

Everyone was edgy at work, waiting for a storm. I left right on time and called Josh telling him I was not going to "do" anywhere without my dog. He met me at my door telling me I was smart, and we could go together.

"It's going to start snowing, you're driving!" I snapped. I was not excited about walking around a strange neighborhood with a storm coming. I remembered my new key chain and put on an extra layer of clothes, slipping a few heavy bean bags in my pockets. Can't stay home and hide every time it storms in a Minnesota winter or you'll suffer from cabin fever, but no sense being stupid either.

I had to trek across the road to gather my dog at Mindy's. Mindy was distracted by her paperwork and wished me luck without even looking up.

It felt better wandering around Beth's neighborhood with Lady Friend sniffing everything and enjoying herself in a very doggy fashion. Susan's house was shut tight with the lights off so we split up. Josh headed north and I headed for the next house south of Susan's.

It was cloudy, and the sunset was more of a fading glow than an actual sunset, but dark would be upon us quickly. I knocked at the door and a thin woman in several layers of dressing gown answered the door.

"What can I do for you?" she asked looking at Lady Friend suspiciously. "Not a good night to be passing out pamphlets or spreading the word."

"Not doing either," I responded. "Just wondering if you would be willing to talk about your neighbors?"

"Funny!" she said laughing. "Nobody has ever knocked on my door asking for gossip before."

I tilted my head inquiringly.

She laughed. "You are letting out the heat, might as well come in and gossip over coffee," she stepped back and motioned me in. "But, if you try to sell me anything, you'll be on your seat in the snow."

I nodded and stomped the snow off my boots and stepped out of them. I followed her into a warm, welcoming kitchen in my stocking feet. Lady Friend sat on the doorstep and I let her stay outside.

"Nice house," I commented.

"I like it," she replied, pouring a couple of cups of coffee from an old-fashioned drip coffee pot. Oh, my, I would be up all night with that brew.

"So, tell me about your neighbors," I said, sitting at the in-kitchen table.

"You are a subtle as a bear in the spring," she replied and put some cookies on a plate.

I shrugged. She was right, I was a bit blunt. I know some people think subtle is helpful in customer service. They are wrong. Getting to the issue quickly and gently is important as well as understanding the issue and offering solutions. Offering solutions and caring are really the only secrets.

"Any particular neighbors you are interested in? She asked.

I shook my head. I was looking for straight answers and shooting in the dark. I did not want to ask about Beth and Ben directly.

"Well, not that I watch out my windows for fun, you understand," she continued. "But, that widow Cid is on the prowl almost all the time. I swear he is interested in every woman on the street. Not that Ben the Real Estate Agent is any different, but Ben has a wife. There was a bit of drama the other day over there. Lots of police cars and men in suits walking around. I even heard there was a murder there." She leaned forward. "I head Ben Sanders was killed, in his own kitchen!"

I nodded. None of this was new except for Cid the widower.

"But how could that be," she continued pensively. "I swear I've seen Ben skulking about since then."

I sat up with that and put my cookie down. This was new.

"What?" I frowned. "I'm pretty sure they arrested his wife for the murder. Kind of needed a body for that."

"Maybe it was his ghost," she said, smiling a mysterious grin. "I would love to see that creep reduced to a wispy shadow of himself."

I shook my head. This was not getting clearer, only more clouded like the weather rolling in. I finished my cookie and drank down the strong, bitter coffee. I was going to need some energy to face the storm.

"Thanks for the coffee and conversation," I said getting ready to leave.

"My dog is afraid to go that way on walks," she continued. "Proof of supernatural goings-on."

"So true," I lied, stepping back into my boots and tightening the laces. I wanted out of this house and I wanted out now. I did not believe she saw the ghost of the dead man. It was more likely she saw his secretive brother that only a few seemed to even know about. Not that I discounted that there might be more that we knew. I just didn't want to think about it being in my neighborhood.

I walked a short distance and realized Josh was walking next to me with Lady Friend. He raised his eyebrows in a question and I responded with a snort, "Another strike for the newbie."

"How so?"

"Well the widow Cid is on the prowl and she thinks she saw the ghost of Ben Sanders skulking about."

"Interesting. Good job."

"Really?" I snapped. "This is getting murky and murkier."

"Is murkier even a word?" he asked.

"Probably not, can we go now?"

"Well door-to-door usually involves more than one door at a time."

I glared at him. "I'm tired and a storm is coming."

He shrugged and headed for his car parked at the little park on the lake. I saw a shadow and movement out of the corner of my eye and started towards it. Josh grabbed my arm.

"Chasing shadows in the dark is not good investigative work," he murmured and directed me to the door of his car. I climbed in muttering and Lady Friend clamored into the back seat, her tail wagging.

"I thought you liked taking risks and chasing shadows in the dark," I said to him.

"Yup, I do," he replied, grinning at me. "But it's not your style. And a storm is coming."

The snow started in earnest and the wind was picking up as we drove the short distance around the lake. Even without driving I could feel the car being pushed around by the wind. Josh was keeping to the road, but it was work even with his heavy car. He stopped in front of Mindy's house as it was on the same side of the road as we were and I jumped out with Lady Friend quickly. He was moving forward as soon as I slammed the door, not wanting to get stuck with the new snow blowing over the road.

"Good thing I don't need to work tomorrow," I said to Lady Friend.

She whined, and I looked where she was looking. There, standing in the swirling snow, was Guy. Just standing there. I started walking towards him, but Lady Friend pushed against my legs.

"No chasing shadows in the dark?" I asked her. She whined again.

"Fine," I snapped, putting my hand on her back. Then turning back to the space that no longer held a figure I yelled into the storm, "You have to either be more helpful or stop bringing me problems!"

Mindy's door opened and Mindy yelled at me. "Stop yelling at the storm, it does no good!"

Warm, yellow light spilled out around her and we hurried to her door.

Chapter Seventeen

Gabriela and a Cartful of Stuff

Saturday morning dawned with a new snow-scape. It was quite pretty in the morning light with the trees covered and the unbroken swirls of snow drifts.

Today would be a good day to pick up a few things at Walmart and see if the infamous Gabriela was working and in the mood to talk.

I drove through the winter wonderland to the Walmart by my work. It was a bit out of the way but that was the one Gretchen spoke to Gabriela at. I sent Josh a quick text as I promised to keep him aware of anything I did and enjoyed the drive.

I wandered the aisles, avoiding running into anyone; this was a busy store and I never really understood the layout. Seems like the aisles ran into each other and conspired to get me shopping for things I don't need.

After gathering an entire cartful of stuff I didn't need, I spotted the elusive Gabriela clerking at the checkout. I wondered if she confided in her supervisor here about her past. Why she decided to tell an entire class of trainees during an ice breaker that she was afraid of her son was still a mystery to me. And then ask if they thought it was because she shot his father—in front of him, ten years ago. What was she thinking?

I waited in the longer line to have her check me out and watched her work. She still had the air of mystery and the uncanny ability to look perfect. She was small and overdressed for the job in black silk pants to go with a white, fitted silk shirt. The Walmart vest over that shirt looked rough and common.

"Find everything you need?" she asked without looking at me.

"Hi, Gabriela," I said smiling.

She looked up and I made the effort to look her in the eyes and waited for a reaction.

I was not disappointed. She started a little and pulled her head back a tiny bit. I had the impression she would have stepped back but was determined not to. That was interesting.

"How's it going?" I asked quietly. Doesn't hurt to be polite and let things develop on their own.

She shrugged and looked down at the items on the belt. She started putting them through the scanner.

I didn't have much time.

"A man named Penn Sanders told me you recommended him for a job," I murmured.

She continued to look down at the items on the belt but smiled a tiny, secret smile. Okay, so she did know a Penn and this amused her.

"Would he fit in our team for customer service?" I inquired.

She started and looked up at me again. "Penn would never apply for a mundane job and he would be much more than you could handle."

I raised my eyebrows and replied, "I managed you and you were a handful."

"Yeah, but he's different."

"How?"

"Mean—" she stopped and looked away. "If you are smart you will stay away from him."

"Are you smart?"

"No. Stay away from him."

"I can't find him."

"No? He'll find you if you keep asking about him."

My order was rung up and she told me that I spent sixty-three dollars and ten cents. I didn't even really know what I bought. I put my card through the machine and she waited quietly looking everywhere but at me.

"Tell him for me," I said quietly. "He isn't going to get away with it."

She paled suddenly, which was scary because it was so quick. I suddenly felt sorry for this woman I had considered a troublemaker until right now.

"There is help," I started.

She interrupted, "No." She turned her gaze to the next customer and smiled.

I took my bags of sixty-three dollars and ten cents worth of stuff and walked away slowly. Maybe she was a troublemaker when she worked for me, but she was so sad it made me depressed and she was way too proud to ask for help.

It was pretty and sunny through the cold on the drive home with my stuff, but I was too pensive to enjoy it much. Getting home, I sent a report to Josh with a note containing the pitiful information I got from questioning Gabriela, and the fact that Find my iPhone showed a third phone under Ben's name being used and moving around. It was not much, but it was someone else besides Beth claiming there was a Penn and he sounded like a real gem among gems.

Chapter Eighteen

Doctored Tea and a Broken Window

Amongst the assorted stuff I got from Walmart was red spray paint. After a light lunch of an apple and banana, I decided over zero was warm enough for spray paint and painted the nasty graffiti on my garage door over with a bright red. I also did the front door. The paint would not last as it would need to cure in warm weather, but it would cover the ugliness until spring when I could paint for real.

Josh pulled into the driveway honking his horn and grinning.

I was so not in the mood to talk to him. Or anyone else for that matter. I just wanted out of this absurd part-time job that didn't pay. Everyone I talked to was either awful or pitiful, and the ugliness was following me home. I like to surround myself with positive things, not the negative, violent mood that was swirling around me.

"What?" I asked aggressively.

He just laughed.

"I'm glad all this is amusing to you," I muttered.

"Invite me in, offer me tea and we can talk," he countered politely.

Fine. He is a nice young man. I could have a cup of tea and warm up.

He stomped his feet at the front door and removed his boots. Okay, he was a nice young man with manners.

"I want to meet your wife," I said. "I bet she's interesting and full of life."

I made peppermint tea with honey and added a new twist. I have discovered an addition to tea other than brandy—whiskey, Knob Creek with maple. Very mellow and potent.

"Our defense is now convinced there is a Penn, and the police have admitted they found three different common fingerprints at their house and so they believe there were three living there," he said sipping his drink and raising his eyebrows into his hairline. "This is dangerous," he added tipping his drink towards me.

"Tea without help is a bit bland," I replied.

"Heaven forbid a nice, little lady drink bland."

"I am not a nice, little old lady!" I retorted sharply.

He just grinned a lopsided grin. "No," he agreed. "You are not old."

"Nor little," I murmured.

Again, the robust laugh. He was starting to get on my nerves.

"Your research has convinced the defense and I that there is a brother and I am searching other databases to find evidence of a brother, specifically a twin." Josh took a deep breath and concluded, "This will help the defense."

"What about the truth?" I retorted. "Don't you want the truth or justice?"

"I would like a little truth," he responded. "Truth is clarity. Justice is a dream and an impossible goal."

"I might have some chocolate chip cookies to go with the tea," I offered, an olive branch.

"Of course, you do," he grinned and held out his mug for a second cup of tea.

Oops, more than one of those and he shouldn't drive. Oh, well, I didn't have any plans and I could drive him home.

"More tea and cookies but you need to give me your keys."

"When I was a beat cop, I didn't believe there were people like you," he responded, his voice quiet and almost a whisper.

"Like me?" I bristled. "Naïve and wandering around in the dark?"

I gave him a second cup of tea and a plate of fresh cookies, snatching one for me and holding out my hand for his keys.

He shook his head seriously but before he could say anything, Lady Friend started growling at the window. I stepped away.

The front window shattered, and I pushed myself further into the corner of the kitchen by the refrigerator. This part-time, unpaid job was costing me a lot of money. I wondered what the deductible was on the second window to shatter in a year.

Josh moved quickly out the side door and I called Lady Friend to me. I didn't want to be alone in the kitchen, nor did I want to go anywhere.

She came to me and stood between me and the window. Her hair was bristled on top and she watched the dark opening like me, but she growled low in her throat. I shivered in my stocking feet and crouched down pulling her into me.

Josh returned talking on his cell in wet, stockinged feet.

"Man in a light-blue ski jacket took off in something small, dark, and well powered." he commented. I wasn't sure if it was directed to me or whomever he had on the phone.

"Let me get you some dry socks," I said, standing and running to the laundry room.

"Thanks," he said, putting them on. "Then we need to put plywood up until you can get a glazer in here to replace the glass. Don't want to freeze the pipes."

I assumed he had already called 911 so I made a couple of calls too and found a man who would come out in an hour. Josh wandered the room and then went outside, this time with his boots, to take pictures with his phone. He didn't talk while he worked, and it was soothing. I guess I stirred a pot today and I was glad not to be alone.

"Bill the attorney for the repair," Josh said suddenly, marking a spot on the opposite wall. "That is, if you don't want to bill your home insurance."

I nodded, speechless.

"Come here," he said quietly. I walked over and he showed me a hole in the wall. "This looks like a slug," he said. "Someone is not happy with our involvement."

I nodded again, wondering how hard it was going to be to repair the wall.

I started to touch it and he grabbed my hand shaking his head. "Don't touch until the police have finished," he said. "And we are stopping your involvement immediately."

"Will that make me safe?"

"Probably not."

"Then we better finish."

"I like risks, you don't," he said.

"No, but I don't like being bullied either," I replied.

Chapter Nineteen

Bail for Beth And Swimming in the Snow

My home was still swarming with police when the glazer came. They allowed him to start work to replace the glass.

"Have an inclination to come with me and talk to Beth?" Josh asked.

I glared at him. He would have his little private chats with his old police buddies and get the inside scoop, but I would be left out. I ground my teeth together and glared at him. This was not making my personality nicer. He just smiled.

I left Lady Friend in the bedroom with the door closed and asked the glazer if he would lock the door when he left. He laughed and said the cops would probably still be mucking around tracking up my house when he left. But he would send me the final bill.

We bundled up and left in Josh's car.

But Beth was not in holding. The duty officer told us that bail was posted and she left. He did not know who posted the bail, it was a local bail bondsman.

I was stunned. Can someone post bail for you if you don't want it posted? Where was Beth and was she in danger were the two questions I had for the duty officer. He just looked at me askance and Josh pulled me away.

"We need to talk," he said.

"Beth refused bail because she was afraid," I whispered rather loudly. "How could they force her to be released when she instructed no bail? Was she released to someone who will hurt her?"

"We don't know that is what happened," he started in a reasonable tone.

"We don't know that is not what happened," I returned in a strident tone. "What can we do to protect Beth?"

"Let's stop at a couple of local bail bondsmen and see if they know who and how."

"Which one?"

"Good question," he replied. "I know a couple personally and I know they aren't very forthcoming with their records."

He looked at me and could probably see the panic in my eyes.

"Better idea," he said. "How about I take you home and go talk to the attorney and see what he thinks?"

"Sure, why not?" I agreed. "Can we stop somewhere and get a stun gun and body armor?"

He raised his eyebrows. "You're making a joke, right?"

"Only sort-of," I whispered. I was really worried about Beth, but I didn't have a clue what I could do to help.

We drove to my home quietly, both of us planning our next move. I was considering moving out of the state.

The house was dark and I started to get out.

Josh put his hand on my arm to stop me.

"What?"

"I want to remind you, I showed the police what looked like a slug embedded in your kitchen wall."

"That's what you said."

"It will have to be tested and I don't know if they will tell us the results, but it looked like a high-powered rifle shot."

"What? You didn't say that!"

"Be careful, is all I'm saying," he responded. "I want you to continue to work for me and I might even start paying you. But," he continued raising his eyebrows, "this case is finished for us. We have raised significant doubt not only to Beth being the killer but also to who was murdered. Our job is done."

"Except the part about Beth and danger," I muttered.

"Yeah, except that part," he agreed.

I gave him my best manager glower and turned to go in.

"Be careful," he repeated.

Yeah, like I needed that repeated.

I went in the house hoping that the doctored tea I gave Josh was still on the kitchen table. It was and I downed the cold tea and whiskey in one gulp. I followed it with a couple of decadent cookies and made a second cup.

"Now what?" I muttered to myself. The only answer I got was Lady Friend whining to be let out of the bedroom.

"Poor baby!" I crooned, opening the door, hugging her and letting her kisses soothe me.

She then went to the side door to the garage and whined.

"If you want out," I murmured. "Why not the front or back door? They go directly outside."

She leaned on the door and looked at me. I so wished she could talk right at that moment. Why was this door preferable?

"Look," I said opening the door. "Just the garage—no way out unless the garage door is open."

She barreled out and ran to the corner and there was a crumpled heap that could be a person. My heart moved into overtime and was beating so hard it was hard to hear anything else. Lady Friend was licking the lump and I ran over in spite of my pounding heart.

What if this was someone who was planning on hurting us, what if this was a person who was hurt? Even worse, what if this was a body?

Every possibility that ran into my head seemed worse than the one before.

The lump moved and I reached Lady Friend. Sitting on the floor of my garage was Beth Sanders.

"Why are you dressed like that and why are you in my garage?" I sputtered.

"Someone bailed me out and I don't know who," she replied, her hand on Lady Friend. "I can't go home and I don't want to freeze and . . ."

"Come inside," I offered. "I'm pretty sure my garage is not a good place to hide out."

"Do you know any good places?" she asked.

"How much cash do you have?"

"None," she replied.

"Need cash to hide, I'm pretty sure," I muttered. "But, will hiding solve your problem?"

"He will always be out to get me."

"Which he?"

"Does it matter?"

"Sort of, yes," I mumbled, still distracted. "You really need to know what you're running from."

Lady Friend started growling low in her throat. I listened and I could hear talking in my backyard. I could not make out the words but they were harsh and low. Why would anyone be in my yard? Without another thought, the visceral need to listen to Lady's instinct took over.

"We run," I agreed suddenly, "but we do it my way."

I grabbed my purse and coat and ran out to the car, followed closely by Beth and Lady Friend. I saw someone jimmying the back door and I decided to let them search the house. It would give us time.

I jumped in my Saturn and started her up before Beth had the door closed.

"Seatbelts!" I hissed and gave her as much power as I could and still be quiet. This was not how I usually treated my poor little car. She wasn't designed for high speed chases or fast getaways and coughed a little, giving off an exhaust smell.

"Sorry, Baby," I whispered, patting the dashboard.

"Don't drive so fast!" Beth gasped.

"Why not? Maybe a nice cop will stop me to give me a ticket and I can swear at him and get locked up."

"Good idea," she returned.

"No," I snorted. "It is not a good idea! It's sarcasm!"

Since I didn't see anyone following us, I decided we had a clean get away and we needed cash to run. I pulled into the bank's drive-through and stuck my card into the machine. I requested two hundred dollars and put in my pin. The money slid into the slot and I was reaching for it when Beth screamed.

Right behind us was a huge grey van and it was coming fast. I grabbed the cash and gunned my poor little car. She is little and deceptively responsive, she went around the building in a nice, tight turn. The van swerved and scraped the light pole. That gave us enough time to get on the road and moving. This was my neighborhood, I was not in the mood to have an ugly van drive my pretty little car off the road and hurt Beth. Okay, maybe they would hurt me also, but I wasn't willing to think about that possibility. Lady Friend was still growling low but otherwise staying in the back seat. Beth appeared to be hyperventilating but I couldn't be sure.

I took the next left very sharply and then another left. In just two blocks was a police station and that seemed like the best designation to me. My little car coughed a few more times but she kept going. I pulled into the parking lot and laid on the horn. The van slowed but immediately sped back up and took off. One of the police cars already had an occupant and it followed the van. I hoped they would catch it, but I didn't expect it.

I did expect a crowd of the good guys to come streaming out the of building but that didn't happen either. It was quiet, very quiet. I started to open the door and Beth reached over suddenly calm.

"Don't get out, don't stay here, please," she breathed.

"Why?"

"I'm scared."

I pulled out my phone. I called my husband first and told him someone was chasing me and I didn't want to go home. He told me to come to his work.

Actually, that was a good idea. He was in programing but he worked for a German bank. I was betting they had pretty good security.

I drove towards his office, staying at the speed limit and watching for anyone following me. I asked Beth to use my phone to call Josh. When his recording came on, I told him that Beth was with me and someone tried to run us off the road. I asked his voicemail to call me back. Good thing I already had a plan. Waiting for someone to return a message while fight or flight instincts were in full force was not going to work.

I was looking forward to getting into a high-security building. I got onto the freeway and set the speed control. The road was still a little wet from last night's snow but didn't seem too slippery.

The snow scape changed to fewer houses and more snow-covered trees. It doesn't take long to get out of the city in St. Paul, Minnesota. It was starting to get dark and the farms looked idyllic and the lights in the houses and barns glowed yellow.

A bump against my rear bumper startled me. I looked in the rear-view mirror and there was that clunky, gray van. How did I miss that? More importantly, what was I going to do about it?

"Call 911," I yelled to Beth.

"On your phone?" she questioned.

"I don't care!" I snapped back.

She hesitated, and the van bumped us, making my poor little Saturn start to slide on the wet road.

I steered in the opposite direction, keeping my steering as calm as possible. Everyone who survives long in the frozen North knows that only calm, slow, counter reactions will keep you on the road. The van was swaying and trying to stay on the road also.

"Call 911 right now," I growled gritting my teeth.

"Ben says calling the cops makes things worse," she replied flatly.

"Ben is dead!"

She picked up my phone. "Says you," she muttered.

"Call 911, or I'm stopping and letting you out," I may have actually hollered.

"You can't just stop in the middle of a freeway," she argued.

"Watch me!" I grunted as I braked as hard as I dared. The van barreled past us, weaving for control.

I sat in the middle of the freeway with cars streaming past on either side. Several of them honked. Must be newcomers to Minnesota. True Minnesotans don't honk.

I grabbed my phone and punched in 911. I told them I was on 35E going North and that a grey van was reckless and trying to hit me as calmly as I could. My voice only shook slightly as I requested assistance. They asked what exit I was close to and told me to stay put.

Through luck and the skill of several drivers behind me, I made it to the shoulder. I put the car into Park and turned to Beth.

"Either help me help you," I said quietly. "Or get out and face those crazies alone."

"Sorry," She murmured looking down.

I felt like I kicked a puppy.

"Darn!" I muttered opening my phone again. That shows you how upset I was.

I called Josh again and left another voicemail telling him what exit we were close to and asking him to please join us.

I called my husband again and left a voicemail for him also. At least if the inhabitants of the grey van came back and killed us there were plenty of voicemails to check.

Headlights came through the rear window and Beth started to get ready to get out.

"No wait," I whispered suddenly. "Keep your seatbelt on."

I didn't see the cherry lights reflecting on the wet road. Shouldn't a cop have his or her lights on?

The vehicle shining its headlights in our eyes did not slow but barreled right towards us full speed. I turned the wheel towards the road and kept my foot on the brake.

I heard a sickening crunch as my rear bumper folded in on itself. We spun 90 degrees with our front tires staying on the pavement, but our rear started sinking into the snow-filled ditch.

"Open your window," I yelled as I opened mine.

The van was still accelerating and with an awful, metal-bending squawk it scraped by us and went full speed into the ditch. It flipped and for a completely insane minute I wondered if I should go help them. No, that would be counterproductive to staying alive.

I called 911 once more and told the operator we were in the ditch and so was the van. I told her I was leaving the scene to protect myself. She didn't like it, but I left my phone number. Then Beth and I proceeded to crawl out of my car through the windows, followed by Lady Friend. We headed for the closest exit in a half-run, half-hobble pace.

It was cold and as the fear stopped warming me I realized I was shivering. That quarter of a mile that looked so close when we were driving suddenly looked far away. Beth must have had the same feelings because I heard her sigh. Little flakes of snow started to blur the view and I almost swore.

"Really? Mother Nature!" I yelled into the sky. A blue flash of lightning was her only response. That replaced the frustration with a new, real fear. A winter storm with lightning was never a storm you wanted to be out in. It was going to get much worse and probably soon.

"Gotta keep going!" I yelled to Beth and she nodded. Lady Friend pushed against me and I agreed with her. Now would be a good time to get out of the weather.

"Can you run a little?" I asked Beth and she nodded again.

I ran in the snow on the side of the freeway with Beth and Lady Friend. I always told my kids that to get me to run someone had to be chasing me. I really wished that saying had not come true and I really wished I had let them push me into exercising more. I was breathing hard in moments, but I was warmer. Maybe I could handle a slow run if I focused on breathing.

I could hear Beth breathing hard also so we slowed a little, but we were still jogging.

It seemed like we were making good progress but when I looked over my shoulder to check if we were being chased, I slipped and slid down the incline of the ditch feet first. The snow got under my coat in the slide and it was a sharp, wet, prickly feeling. I stopped sliding at the bottom of the ditch with my heart pounding and waist deep in snow. My legs were stuck in snow but my arms were free. My feet were so cold I wasn't sure I could still feel them.

It was a short distance in reality, but the five feet of slippery, snow-covered hill between me and the freeway was looking like it went on forever.

I looked at Beth who was wringing her hands and watched my dog slide down to join me. She whined once and tried to push me forward. I let her pull me into a crawling position and started to half-swim, half-crawl up the hill. Lady Friend kept pace with me. All I could think of was to put one hand in front of the other and keep moving. I slid back once but still I was closer to the road than a few moments before. Every part of my body was wet and Lady Friend would not let me give up. I considered curling up in a ball and hiding. That was not the smart part of my brain.

So many other thoughts went through my mind at this time. It was so far up that hill. But, if I stopped would I ever see my grandbabies? Come to think of it, would I ever have grandbabies? Why wasn't Beth coming to help? Why was she running but unwilling to talk? Why did someone take my involvement so personally and threatening? Who was that someone? And what was it about this dog that made her smarter than me? She licked my face yet again and I realized I was almost to the road.

Beth reached down to give me a hand and I only hesitated a moment. Why did she wait until now? Would she really help me? She braced herself and pulled, helping me get the final foot and up on my feet. I was shivering uncontrollably.

"Inside," I croaked. "We have to get inside." There did not seem to be any activity behind us. Were the men in the van trapped and freezing? I pushed the guilt away. It was not my problem, not my fault someone rammed us and flipped themselves into the ditch.

Beth took the lead going up the exit ramp. Right there at the top was the most derelict bar I had ever seen.

We burst into light and noise. It was heavenly. Okay, it was dirty, loud, and cheap. I loved it at the moment. They didn't even seem to notice or care we had a dog with us.

"Sit anywhere," a harassed looking young man with a tray of drinks hollered at us. If he wasn't serving beer I would have put him at sixteen tops. He had a mop of uncontrolled blond hair going every direction. He was scrawny and his face looked like it never needed a shave.

"All the way under the table," I said, pushing Lady Friend out of sight. I took off my wet coat and sat down. I no longer cared if someone was chasing me. I wanted something warm to heat me from the inside out. The wind howled outside and every time the door opened snow blew in with the customers.

"Spill it!" I growled at Beth. "I am not liking this being chased and being afraid. What is going on?"

She looked at her hands, wringing them.

"Honestly?" I yelled. No one noticed. Apparently not even Beth. But the harassed kid scooted over.

"What can I get ya?" He asked. "We are cash only, in advance."

"Classy," I replied. "I want whatever you have that is hot and a hot toddy with it."

"Hot toddy?" he asked.

"Never mind," I yelled. "Bring us whiskey and soup or chili."

"Chili we got!" he yelled happily. "Whiskey we got!"

I handed him a twenty from my recent trip to the cash machine. He just looked at it. I gave him a second twenty.

"That'll get you two bowls of chili and two whiskeys."

"What a deal!" I murmured but no one heard or at least, no one acknowledged the comment.

I pulled out my phone from my sodden coat. It was dark and heavy feeling. In an optimistic move I tried to switch it on, but there was no spark of life. I stared at it almost in shock. How could my phone die on me? How could it die on me now?

"Must have gotten wet when you slid into the ditch," Beth murmured helpfully.

"Let me borrow yours," I replied holding out my hand.

"I don't have it," she whispered, almost as if she was afraid of my reaction.

Great, I kicked the puppy and she was afraid of me now.

I so wanted to quit this stupid ride right now. Why help someone who doesn't help themselves at least a little? It's like swimming in snow—slow, cold, and deceptively dangerous.

Our chili and glasses of whiskey were dropped on the table and the harassed young man was gone. The glasses looked dirty and foggy. I just couldn't face the fire that was sure to be in the glass. I was too cold. The chili was hot and steamy and I took a taste. Yup, spicy enough to probably be safe.

I took a couple of greedy bites and started a burning in my mouth that moved down. It slowed the shivers a lot. But it was a bit too spicy so I slowed down.

"Eat," I mumbled around my mouthful to Beth. "Everyone deserves a last meal."

She was used to taking orders so she started to nibble the chili. Like me, she just looked at the glasses of whiskey.

"You drinking that?" asked a rough voice behind me.

"No," I said around food in my mouth. "Take it if you want."

"Don't mind if I do," replied the deep voice. I finally focused on something other than warming up and my bowl of spice with a few beans thrown in. A huge mountain of a man sat next to me, dwarfing the table and the space. I watched the wooden chair wobble a little. He made it look delicate and breakable. He had his head wrapped in a bandana and was dressed in jeans that had seen better days, several layers of mountain-man-plaid shirts and a leather vest. In other words, he screamed biker dude. He tipped up my glass and emptied it into his mouth. I watched a huge Adam's apple bob with swallowing and my drink was gone. That was kind of impressive. He put the glass back on the table with exaggerated gentleness.

Beth nudged her glass to him and he raised his eyebrows. She returned the look and I swear I saw him wink at her once. I was speechless. This is a new feeling for me and I decided to eat chili and enjoy it.

I scraped the bottom of my bowl and looked at Beth's barely touched bowl. I glanced at her still staring at the human mountain and switched bowls with her. My stomach was in charge right now and I wasn't arguing.

That's when my nightmare decided to join the party. Two bloodied men burst into the room and I swore they were going to run in and end us right there. Unfortunately for them, there was a man the size of a MG convertible sitting between us making moon eyes at Beth.

They were both mean-looking with loose clothing and lean frames. They glared at us as if looks could kill and I was reminded of well trained dogs with no orders. Lady Friend pushed against my legs and growled.

"Got any good ideas?" I whispered to her, ruffling her fur at her neck under the table.

"Hey!" thundered the tiny kid with the serving tray. "No dogs in here."

"Yeah!" I replied. "Make them go!"

The gargantuan next to me broke eye contact with Beth and picked up her glass of whiskey.

"Go away!" he bellowed at the two twigs. "These ladies are getting me drunk." Now there is a basis for a new relationship for Beth. At this point I wasn't sure I cared.

To my complete surprise they backed out.

"Friends of yours?" our giant asked before emptying Beth's glass.

"No," I replied.

"They're trying to kill us," Beth said in a whispery voice.

"Hang with me," he said, pushing the empty glass around.

"Want more?" I asked. Maybe he could scare the men chasing us away but now I wanted to be away from him. My mom always told me to never be with someone I couldn't beat up or run away from.

I help up my hand with two fingers and two more whiskeys came over with the kid. He took a twenty and breathlessly told me to keep my dog quiet or he would be in trouble. Lady Friend was fine now, resting her head in my lap and keeping the rest of herself under the table. She seemed fine with the Mountain Man, even if I was uncomfortable.

"Call us a cab," I replied.

He nodded, his blond hair flopping around and disappeared.

I watched the two glasses of whiskey disappear like water into the Mountain Man. He then turned to me and said, "I'm the taxi service around here. Where can I take you?"

"Somewhere safe," Beth whispered. I shook my head.

"I want to stay alive," I muttered stroking Lady Friends head. "And," I shrugged, "wouldn't want you to lose your license for driving after four whiskeys."

He nodded. "You two are classy bitches," he growled. "In trouble but still worried about me."

I didn't disabuse him of this impression. And I didn't even consider calling him on referring to us as bitches. I like female dogs and judging by Lady Friend, they're apparently smarter than me. I just didn't think getting into a car driven by a drunk behemoth was an improvement in our situation.

He looked at me, "You're wet," he observed. "And it's going to storm worse before it's better."

"I noticed," I replied.

"I own this place," he continued. "My room is above us." He gave me a quick look over. "You're the same size as my old lady. Let's get you warm and you can pay her for some clothes and a hot bath. Then you can run again."

"See," I said to Beth as he pulled all 400 pounds of muscle into a standing position. "Running and hiding takes money."

I thought I saw the shadow of a smile under all that beard as he lumbered towards the back, but I couldn't be sure. Beth scuttled after him and I decided a bath, dry clothes, and maybe a working phone to rent would be a huge improvement. In reality, I could handle myself better than Beth and she was already going.

It's like that old saying: "You don't have to be faster than a bear, you just have to be faster than the people hiking with you." Maybe being on the run was going to have a negative impact on my overall personality. I decided to worry about that later, after I was warm.

Chapter Twenty

Warmth is Decadent

We followed Mountain Man through a dark hallway to a rickety set of wooden stairs. They were thick, solid wood that had never seen a paint brush or wood stain. They were stained with other substances at irregular intervals. I didn't want to think about exactly what the stains were. The stairs groaned and creaked at his heavy footfalls.

"Are you sure?" I hissed grabbing Beth's arm.

"Yup," she said, smiling.

I followed with Lady Friend, my heart beating in my throat. I just did not see a viable alternative than trust this man whose body and smell kept screaming, "Run Away!" At least Lady Friend didn't hate him. He probably smelled like another dog to her.

He rapped on the door and opened it. Inside was one of the sweetest apartments I've ever seen. It was filled with light even though it was storming outside. There was polished wood everywhere and a large woman with a round, smiling face was cooking. At our approach, she looked up through the steam on the stove.

"More strays?" she moaned with a crooked smile that took the sting out of her words.

"Yup," he replied and slapped my butt to get me inside. "Bartender is watering down the drinks again, I have to go make him see the light."

She nodded. "Don't skin your knuckles, I like them whole."

He left with a rumble of an answer that I didn't understand.

When I looked at the woman at the stove I decided she was not my size. She was closer to both Beth and I combined. She had grey hair done up in a loose bun on her head. Her eyes were a sharp green and her face was round with smile wrinkles. I started shivering again and she came around from behind the stove.

"What are you doing wet in this weather?" she asked me sternly.

I was shivering too hard to answer but if she called me silly woman I was planning on losing it.

"I have a bag of clothes in the closet I was going to give to Goodwill," she said considering. "Let's put that, and you, in the bathroom with a hot bath."

I nodded. That sounded divine.

"Don't come out until you're warm and dry." With that she shoved me into a well-lit bathroom, complete with a huge tub and a heat lamp. Lady pushed her way into the room with me and our hostess nodded at her.

"Smart dog," she continued. Then she left, turning on the heat lamp and I locked the door behind her.

I started some water filling the huge tub and stripped all the wet, cold clothes off me. I noticed some angry red spots on my legs and stomach, but I didn't care. Warm was all I wanted. I stepped into the warm bath and waited for the shivers to stop. Eventually they did and I added more hot water to the tub. Looking around through the steam I decided this was a bathroom designed for a large person. The tub was huge, and I was floating around in it. The sink ran the length of the room with two basins and a mirror the length of the room over it. The toilet was bigger than I even knew they made or sold. Everything was done up in blue tile and white accessories. I wanted this bathroom for my own.

After I dried off with a white towel the size of some people's sheets, I dug through the bag of discarded clothes. I found a grey sweatshirt only two sizes too big with only a few stains and huge orange sweatpants with a drawstring to tighten. I even found thick, warm socks that didn't match. I put all my wet clothes in a plastic garbage bag that she thoughtfully left on top of the Goodwill bag, except my boots. I put them under the heat lamp and cleaned up the tub.

Now, I needed access to a working phone. My voicemails must have gotten some attention by now.

There was a gentle rap on the door. "We're not alone," whispered my new best friend who was not my size.

Lady Friend didn't seem stressed out, so I slowly opened the door to see Josh sitting at the kitchen table.

"Good look for you," he drawled sipping from a big ceramic cup.

"Shut up," I snapped. "Dry is the new sexy and don't you forget it."

The room filled with his delighted roar of laughter and he pointed his cup at me.

"Touché," he replied. Then he sobered faster than a flash of blue lightning. "What are you doing putting this gentleman and his beautiful lady in harm's way?"

"Shooting in the dark," I muttered honestly.

He nodded.

"Good aim," was his response but he was smiling at the woman who gave me clothes. He turned to me, "I was able to tell you came into this establishment from your tracks and the bear running the bar sent me up here. I also called a tow truck and explained the situation to the police who were upset you left the scene."

I started to respond with a flash of anger and frustration but he held up his hand and for once I just shut up. I must be sick or something.

"Got a destination in mind," he drawled. "Or are you careening in the dark there also?"

"My husband is working at a German bank in the back-office programming," I replied. "I think their security is top notch."

"Won't he be in trouble letting you in?"

"No," I shrugged because I was not positive. "I think he's in charge of their cyber security. They trust him."

He stared at me a second.

"Maybe he can say we are consultants," I continued.

Josh barked with laughter again and I decided that anger was a wonderful way to warm up. I could feel my face turning red and I felt a hot surge of indignation shooting from my core up to the top of my head and down to my toes.

"I have a better idea," he drawled, suddenly serious, cutting off my eminent explosion. I nodded for him to continue.

"Let's use my friends at the station to get Beth to a safe house and you to your home with me making sure it's secure."

"They know where I live," I growled.

"Yup, and I need to catch them to stop this."

"Again! You want me to be bait again!"

"More like still, but yes, a lamb to slaughter."

A muttered curse came from my mouth but no coherent words.

"What choice do you have?" he continued reasonably. "Put your husband and his job at risk or trust your partner?"

"Partner?" I growled. "More like chief annoyance and taskmaster."

"Great basics for a partnership," he agreed.

"You really think I would be putting him or his job at risk?" I muttered a cold nugget of doubt in my stomach.

He nodded and smiled at our hostess who was adding more hot coffee to his cup.

"Fine," I snapped and held out my hand for his phone. "I better make it out of this alive."

"Or else?" He smiled, raising his one eyebrow.

"Or I'll haunt you for the rest of your life, you'll never have sex with your new wife without me floating overhead."

"Now that is a picture," he said dryly, handing me his phone.

I nodded unenthusiastically and texted my husband, "Change of plan, going home and to bed early, no worries." Knowing him, I doubted he would even read my messages until I saw him. He focuses on his work so hard he has been known to forget to come home. I sincerely hoped I was not lying. Josh just gave me an enthusiastic thumbs-up and grinned.

"Have you ever lost a partner?" I asked sweetly.

He didn't answer he just stood up and said, "You coming or do you want to do this alone?"

"Coming," I replied my brain in overload. What was his story? How would it affect me and was he just another liability?

We dropped Beth off with a patrol car that came to meet us. Then Josh drove me home and the house was quiet, but it was a long time before I really relaxed. I could see Josh's car drive by often and a police car also came by every half hour or so. What did I get my customer service butt into? How long before the police got tired of watching my back? I could not think of a way out; the only direction was forward and that scared me.

Chapter Twenty One

Scene at Walmart and an Odd Fight

Sunday morning dawned bright and cold. The roads were already plowed but the trees were still burdened with heavy snow weighing down their branches.

I wasn't alone as a rather concerned husband bundled in with me shortly after I started to drift to sleep. He was determined to sleep wrapped around me. I must have frightened him a little with my phone calls. That was too bad.

"I think I'll wander over to Walmart today after the Apple store and see if Gabriela is working today," I mentioned as I was making toast and eggs.

"Not alone," was his curt comment and it was kind of cute.

"Awww," I said in a low sultry voice. "I think the He-Man likes me." I nuzzled his neck and nipped it.

"Joke all you want," he muttered. "I'm a little worried about what you are doing."

"It is supposed to be just asking questions," I replied. "Someone is not with the program."

"Hummm," he countered wrapping his arm around me. His arms are abnormally long and there was plenty of arm left over to wrap another halfway around me. That made me warm all over.

After clearing the dishes and giving Lady Friend a chance to run around the yard and get some food and water, we bundled up and headed out. I can count the number of times we've shopped together on my fingers. It's not that my husband hates to shop, we just have different styles. I like to wander and check out sales. He likes to zero in on the desired item and procure. Even when we go together we end up separating and meeting at the checkout counter.

This was different. He stuck to me like glue and I could smell the testosterone. This man was in protection mode. It was simple trading in my wet brick for a new phone, all it cost was money. We went in the store together with him literally pressing against my back. I showed them my wet phone and they tried not to laugh.

I had to do an upgrade to get a new phone and then wait while they downloaded my backup from the cloud. I do like the modern technology but sometimes it takes more time than I feel it should. We are so used to things like microwaves we expect immediate results. I wandered the aisles looking at accessories and almost picked out a new, bright pink phone cover when he came around the corner, actually running in the store.

"What?" I said stepping backwards.

"Don't disappear like that," he ordered.

"Whoa, Tex," I said pushing him a step back. "That isn't us, never has been, never will be."

"I'm worried about you," he said.

"I don't blame you," I admitted. "I'm worried myself. But you have to trust me. I trust you to do your dare-devil flying in that tiny plane."

"That is different."

"How?"

"I had training."

"So do I, I have a big, bad PI watching my tail."

"And a lovely tail it is," he said grinning.

"Stop!" I said punching his arm.

He grinned. "I'll do what I can. But that tail is pretty awesome."

I admit it was cute but it was getting a little stale. By the time we made it to Walmart I needed space to breathe. I tried unsuccessfully to distract him with tools and then with household gadgets. Finally, I had enough and in the lingerie department I stopped walking and confronted him, pushing him a few feet from me.

"Stop already!" I hissed.

He shook his head and several ladies stopped what they were doing to stare. Now I was making a spectacle in public, in Walmart for Pete's sake. How low could I go?

"Please!" I added in a strident hiss.

"I don't want to lose you," he growled back at me.

"So you love me enough to drive me to distraction?" I snapped.

"Yes," he yelled. "And I can't imagine not having you in my life!"

Now a crowd was watching and we were having the weirdest fight in our long marriage. I stepped back towards him and whispered harshly, "Not here."

"Yeah," he agreed. "Let's leave and fight somewhere more private." He held onto my elbows and added. "And safer. Let's go somewhere safe."

"Fine," I snapped and twisted away to grab a handful of what was on the table and stormed to the checkout counter.

Gabriela was not at any of the checkout stations. I dropped my handful of undies on the counter and told the young lady I changed my mind and stormed out of the store. I stomped into the parking lot followed by my silent, determined husband. I froze mid-step and he walked into me. I fell forward, and he caught me at the last minute from slamming face first into the snow-covered ground from behind.

"Hey, hey, Spitfire," he breathed into my ear holding me around the waist and pulling me upright. "Take it easy."

I pointed a mitten-covered finger to two men in the parking lot. One looked just like the pictures of Ben Sanders and the other was tall and rail thin.

He reached out and gently lowered my arm.

"Don't point," he whispered. I shivered, and not entirely from the cold.

I just couldn't move and I guess that is a better survival technique than I expected. After a few moments I realized they weren't looking at us. They were talking to each other and laughing. Just like two normal people having fun shopping on a Sunday.

"Those two," I breathed.

"Shh," he responded in my ear. He pulled me closer and just held me tightly, putting his body between me and the men.

Abruptly they both stopped talking and started to scan the parking lot, looking for something. I turned my head into my husband's chest and tried not to panic. He bent his head down, making me feel like I was inside a cocoon.

It must have been an effective camouflage because the two started moving quickly. One opened the car trunk and then they both hefted a large bundle out, dropped it, and jumped into the car. They left the parking lot squealing their tires. I believe we were the only two in the parking lot to even notice.

"555J something," my husband said.

"What?"

"License plate," he muttered.

The large bundle moved a little and I needed to go see. I really didn't want to go see. I dreaded it on a very basic, elemental level.

I started forward and surprisingly he didn't try to stop me. Instead he took out his phone and dialed 911. What did we do before cell phones? I was there, I should remember. But that's what filled my thinking for at least thirty seconds. I think my brain was trying to make me think normally. Nope, not working. But it was somewhat soothing to hear him talking to a dispatcher behind me.

I got to the lump on the cold ground and it was a messed-up Gabriela. She turned her bloody face to me and tried to talk but couldn't. I sat down in the snow and pillowed her head in my lap and screamed.

A hand was on my shoulder and he squeezed. "Please stop, it's okay, the cops are coming."

I tried to stop and breathe, but I could not get enough air. There was blood everywhere but none of it was gushing so I didn't have a clue what I could do to help.

"This could be you," my husband said harshly and that shocked me into breathing. I gave him what I intended as a mean glare. So not the point at this moment in time.

I don't think it worked because he squeezed my shoulder again and murmured, "It's going to be okay."

"For who?" I croaked.

He didn't answer. He just kept rubbing my shoulder.

The police came sooner than I expected, and I was gently pushed aside. I stayed sitting on the ground until they put her in an ambulance.

When my butt started to get cold from the melting snow under it, I slowly got up. I felt, and probably looked, like an old, weary, crippled woman.

The cop who pushed me aside looked at me and raised his eyebrows. I nodded, and he came over.

"I need to know what you saw," he started, pulling out a small recording device. "Do you mind if we record it?"

"No," I said, and he raised his eyebrows again. "No, I don't mind if you record what we say?" I said, tilting my head. I was guessing why he was not happy with just no.

He nodded and cited his name the date and our location. Kristoffer put his arm over my shoulders and stood firm and still. He is my rock, I thought and tried to smile.

"Please state your name, the date, our location and everything you remember seeing," the cop said, pointing the little device toward me.

After giving statements, I asked where they were taking her.

"Hennepin County," he replied. "Why?"

"I came here to talk to her," I replied. "I think she might be willing to open up a little on pain meds."

"Way to be sensitive," Kristoff muttered.

Chapter Twenty Two

Waiting with Brownies and Gabriela Talks

I wanted to drive directly to Hennepin County Hospital but when I texted Josh to tell him where I was going, he was positive we should stay away. He texted that we need to wait behind the lines and let the police question her first.

I could not think clearly as it seemed so personal. Was Gabriela hurt because I talked to her? Was I to blame for her injuries? I didn't even know if she was in an accident or if I was correct and she was beaten half to death. Was this because I told her to tell Penn he would not get away with it? Was this a result of my involvement? And how could I stop when this investigation seemed to have a life of its own?

I could not focus and every time I closed my eyes I saw her blood-covered face.

I texted Josh back and told him I had to do something, and I had to do something now. He was welcome to give me suggestions.

He asked to meet us at the coffee shop around the corner and I went; my overprotective other half came along with no comment.

Josh ambled into the coffee shop to find me half-done with a latte and two chocolate brownies.

Josh raised one eyebrow and Kristoff said, "Stress eating. Gets her every time."

"What?" I mumbled through chocolate. "Want a bite?"

Josh watched me consume another brownie and didn't say anything. When it started to feel awkward having two attentive men watch me stuff my face with chocolate and latte, I slowed down.

"What's next?" I asked Josh. "Still think I should be used as bait?"

Kristoff shook his head and, surprise surprise, so did Josh.

"We need to catch them to stop them," Josh said and I nodded.

"We need to know who they are," Kristoff said.

"Maybe Beth knows," I said. "Maybe Gabriela will talk now."

"Maybe," Josh agreed. "I don't want you taking any chances."

"You would rather I sat around and waited to be alone?"

"No, keep me close," he said.

"And me," said Kristoff. "But I'll trust you."

I got a call at the same time Josh's phone peeped. It was the same cop who took my statement. He wanted me to come to the hospital. Gabriela was awake and told the police to get lost.

"She asked for you," he said. "She said she has a message."

All I could think was how sad that was. She's still doing what she's told even though they were animals. No, animals only fight for reasons that are clear to other animals. My guilty conscience was right—they hurt her because I talked to her.

"Will you protect her?" I asking, also thinking about me. I didn't even listen to the details of the answer. It was in the affirmative was all I cared.

"Coming?" I asked my better half.

"Nah," he said. "I've had enough excitement for today and you're not alone now." He looked right at Josh and Josh nodded. I guess my safety was handed over to another annoying male.

I went with Josh and Kristoff went home by himself in his car. That reminded me that my car was still in the shop being repaired or junked. I really did not want to hear it was totaled because it was my baby. I was still going to drive it, even if the insurance company decided it was totaled.

The hospital was quiet. I let Josh take the lead and we went through the halls that smelled like anesthetic and food. It must be lunch time my stomach told me approvingly, right after that latte and two chocolate brownies at the coffee shop.

We found Gabriela in a room with two police officers. She was half sitting up and now instead of blood everywhere there seemed to be purple bruises. Her left eyebrow was covered with a bandage as well as the eye below it. The sheet and blanket seemed too white and too clean.

"Thanks for comin'," she slurred.

I noticed the cops moving behind her head so that they could hear. I guess I couldn't blame them.

I nodded and sat next to her, trying to make myself take her hand. I started to reach, and she shook her head.

"May be brok'n, lookin' at x-rays."

"God, I'm so sorry," I muttered, leaning close. "Is it my fault they did this?"

"Oh, yeah, you made th'm evil!" she snapped, sounding more like the Gabriela I knew. "I'm alive to give you a message."

"Okay," I whispered, tears running down my face. To think I thought of this tiny person as an evil force, causing Frank to be scared to death.

"Stay away from Penn."

"Did he kill his own brother?" I asked before thinking.

"Don't know," she murmured.

"You dealt drugs, were you dealing for him?" I asked.

"How'd you know tha'?" she slurred.

"Frank told me that's why he wouldn't let you borrow his truck. I wasn't sure, but you just agreed to it."

She looked away.

"Does this have something to do with drugs?" I continued.

"You should leave it be," she replied in a voice that was fading fast. "Too deep," she added. "In too deep."

The hospital drugs seemed to be working, she was drifting and I still had questions.

"Why did Penn kill his brother?" I asked again.

She almost laughed. "You don't let go, do you?"

"No," I replied. I don't.

"Beth's basement," she murmured and then she fell asleep.

I leaned back in my chair watching her chest move with each breath.

This was not just asking questions of the neighbors and Beth. I looked at Josh and he patted my back.

"What a waste!" I muttered.

"We are confident Beth didn't kill her husband," Josh whispered.

"You bastard!" I snapped. That was the equivalent of a nuclear device going off in my soul. I never swear or call people names! Never! Somehow, to my mind, using the fact Gabriele was beat up to prove Beth was innocent was lower than blaming a victim for being attacked. Someone else getting hurt was not the goal and should not be a point in our favor. It bothered me on a fundamental level of what I consider right and wrong.

"Glad to see you're picking up the vocabulary," was his first response. "But for the record, I did not beat her up, I did not get you involved, and I did not make those people evil."

"Take care of her," I said to the cops behind us, pretending not to listen.

"Best we can, ma'am, best we can."

"Please take me home," I said to Josh with as much dignity I could muster. I was still shaking inside, thinking that Gabriele's pain was a tick in our favor.

He nodded and held out his arm as support. I ignored it and headed for his car.

When we got home my sweet, innocent husband was not there.

Lady Friend heard the car approach and decided that was a good time to start howling in the backyard.

"How did she get out?" I asked aloud to myself. I had a sinking feeling about how she got out.

I ran outside with Josh following. In the yard was my beautiful best friend and she was tied to a tree. I untied her while she trembled. She kept whining and pushed against me while I attempted to hold back tears. They would not help right now. Something was very wrong.

"I'm going to Beth's safe house," I announced. I knew something was wrong. Kristoff wouldn't let

Lady Friend out and then leave the house. He just wouldn't. It was cold and she could get lost and he would be out all that money we spent to adopt her. No, he would not do that. Something was wrong.

"I'd better drive as you don't have a car," Josh responded.

I climbed into his car and promptly started shaking. Josh herded Lady Friend into the back seat and started driving.

"Faster," I urged.

"Why? What do you think happened?"

"Nothing good," I replied as I texted my husband.

Chapter Twenty Three

Nothing but Dust Bunnies

"Beth!" I hollered, entering her unlocked safe house without knocking. "This needs to end!"

Silence was the only answer I got. I tried to call and then left another text for my husband.

"Darn it," I muttered starting up the stairs. "You are going to talk to me, and I don't care if you make me feel like I beat up a puppy! I'm ready to beat on puppies!"

My feet made echoing thumps on the stairs. A small bedroom and tiny bathroom were upstairs. The bed was unmade, and the closet was empty of clothes. I checked under the bed and there were lots of dust-bunnies but no Beth and nothing of hers I could see.

The tiny bathroom was done all in blue and yellow. It should have looked cheerful but instead it looked faded and sad. I checked the shower and the tiny linen closet. No Beth, not even a toothbrush.

"Long gone," Josh said standing in the doorway and filling it.

"Tell me something I don't know," I snapped pushing past him.

"This safe house is probably no longer safe," he replied turning to watch me stumble down the stairs.

"No joke, Sherlock!" I snipped.

"Don't go chasing shadows in the dark," he said quietly. "Think."

"Think?" I repeated, trying not to scream.

"What did Gabriela have to say?"

"Nothing new! Stay away! In too deep, Beth's basement!" I was practically blubbering. But we both perked up at the same instant.

"Beth's basement!" we said together.

We ran to Josh's car and I noticed that I hadn't really seen him run before.

Lady Friend jumped in the back seat and I buckled up. It seemed to take forever for Josh to put his key into the ignition and turn it. He backed out slowly and I bounced on my seat saying nothing. I didn't want to distract him. This was taking so long. When he finally got moving forward his huge engine did purr and we moved quickly over the slick road.

I couldn't say why, but Beth's disappearance was making me very worried about my better half. Where was he and why wasn't he at home or answering his phone?

Chapter Twenty Four

Beth and Naomi and a Bat

Beth's house was dark as we skidded up to it. The lake was darker and there was Guy, just standing amid all the dark ice houses. I could tell it was him, despite only being backlit from the dim light of oil lamps coming from under the ice house doors. I got out of the car to run out and demand answers from him, but by the time I shut the car door, he was gone.

Josh thought he saw movement in the trees around the neighbor's yard. He took off at a lope followed by Lady Friend who was silent and intent.

I went to the back door of Beth's house. I did not want to join Josh and chase shadows in the dark. The lock was broken so I told myself it wasn't breaking and entering. The silence was empty of the normal sounds of cars going by and little animals chittering. Maybe it was me not hearing anything not related to finding the answers and my husband.

The house still had a faint copper smell of blood and over it the tingling aroma of cleaning solution.

The air was stale and cool but not freezing. Someone must have turned the heat to low.

I didn't check each room carefully before entering as a good PI would do. No, I ran through the back room, ignoring the maple floors and careful placing of leather furniture. I was looking for a basement. The door to the stairs was in the corner of the kitchen. I stepped around the blood stains and suddenly slowed down. My heavy breathing was making me a little dizzy and it wouldn't do to tumble down in the dark. But it wasn't dark I realized as I started down.

The air was full of incoherent sobs and Beth was huddled in a corner between a foosball machine and a maple and granite bar. Naomi Pyle was standing over her with a baseball bat. Her feminine airs were gone and she was standing with her legs wide and her face a mask of hate.

"You will tell me where you hid them," she said. "You will tell me now, or I'll finish you."

"No, you won't," I said to her back. Did I say that out loud?

She turned around almost in slow motion.

Yup, I said that out loud. I shook my head at my own stupid behavior and pulled out my keychain with pepper spray. What good would a little pepper spray do against a baseball bat?

She swung it around slowly with a sneer on her face. "Little Customer Service Lady," she taunted. "Going to return my deposit?"

"What?"

She charged swinging towards my head. I dropped to the floor and started spraying pepper spray.

She missed my head but got my arm. The pain went straight up my arm and I kicked out.

I got her leg and she stumbled down to the floor with me. I sat up and sprayed pepper spray directly into her face and eyes.

She screamed and came towards me blindly, the bat forgotten. She hit my face and I fell back. She was swinging wildly. I could still see even though my face and arm were throbbing. I scrambled up and grabbed the bat. I tapped her on the butt with it, maybe a little harder than necessary.

"Stay still or I'll hit you in the head!" I yelled.

She froze and turned her face to me. It was blotchy and swelling. Her eyes were swollen closed.

"Beth!" I yelled. She was still in the corner, sobbing.

"Get your sorry butt over her and tie this girl up."

Beth was used to orders, pulled herself together, and tied up Naomi. Then she returned to her corner and curled up into a ball. Great, just great.

"You are both going to talk to me," I said

"You going to offer me something like customer service?" Naomi said facing the wall now instead of me. She was really blinded. I hoped it wasn't permanent. I gave myself a mental slap. That was not what I needed to be thinking about right now.

"Customer service is not about giving away stuff," I replied going into supervisor mode because it was comfortable. "It's about understanding the problem and finding solutions."

"Understand this," she replied. "Penn will kill you and your pretty husband."

"Why?"

"Cause he's like that," Beth put in from her corner.

"What is the problem?" I asked. "Why kill Ben?"

Beth put her head between her legs and whimpered. Really?

"Beth," I said in as patient a voice I could. "Why was Ben killed?"

Beth put her arms over her head and continued to whimper.

"Jeez!" Naomi said her hands clenched into fists. "Stupid woman! It's because you hid Penn's drugs and the money. They're supposed to be here, in this basement."

"How else could I stop Ben from using!" Beth screamed.

"Wait a minute," I said. "I thought you hated Ben and he was abusing you."

"Penn pretended to be Ben and abused her," Naomi said. "She's weak, and Penn likes weak and scared, makes him feel good."

"Why do you still care?" I asked Beth.

But Naomi answered, "But I'm strong and I like money. Penn is going to hurt you."

I was suddenly not so sure I cared if she lost her sight.

"Where?" I asked Beth.

"I don't remember," she replied. "There was blood and—" she stopped unable to breathe.

"And that two-timing bastard went to Gabriela instead of me!" Naomi continued in her own world. I tried to care.

Instead I went to the bar and got a glass of water. I crouched by Beth and got her to drink. You can't sob and drink at the same time. You choke. Beth stopped crying and just looked at me with tears running down her face. "I tried to separate the twins because one of them was nice to me," she said. "He's dead. It's my fault."

"Stop blaming yourself for what others do," I replied. "It's one reason you are abused."

She stared at me like I had an extra nose.

"I hid the drugs to stop him from using," she repeated. "He was killed because he couldn't find them. I ran to find them, I remember now," she continued almost in a monotone. "It was cold and I couldn't find them."

"I thought you didn't believe it was him," I said.

"I don't know who it was," she sniffed. "I don't want it to be him."

"She's abused because she lets it happen," Naomi said still facing the wall.

"It's more complicated than that," I returned, watching Beth.

Beth just cried silently. "What did you do when you found Ben?" I asked again.

She shrugged. "Ran, I ran to get the drugs"

"Why?"

"To save Ben, Penn kept yelling 'Where are they?' "

Stop a minute, my brain said to me.

"You saw Ben murdered?"

"Penn was trying to get to me, again,"

The lake, Beth was wandering out of her mind on the lake.

"Beth," I said quietly. "The lake."

She cowered in the corner, putting her head between her knees. The sobbing returned. I was confused but I couldn't afford to let it break my focus. Something was pounding in the back of my head. "Why did you run out on the lake, and who killed who?"

"I don't know!" she screamed.

"Damn it!" Naomi spat out. "Make her stop!"

"I'd like to make you stop," I replied. "Beth, who killed who and why were you on the lake?"

"They were fighting, I picked up the knife but Ben took it back. I ran to the lake to get the drugs and make them stop fighting. I was going to give up on stopping Ben from using. Just make them stop. But it was cold and I couldn't remember where and then it was too late."

Josh joined us, breathless.

"Where have you been?" I snapped.

"Chasing shadows in the dark, like I told you not to," he replied.

"Beth," I said, pulling her up and wrapping my arm around her. "Can we sign into iCloud right now and see if Penn's phone is near us?"

She nodded still sobbing quietly, and we went up the stairs.

We went into a leather furnished study with a modern office set up. We sat in a couple of cushy rolling chairs and booted up the computer.

Beth's fingers flew over the keyboard and we saw that Penn's phone was close to Clearwater again.

Humm. Good place to look for Penn.

"Cabin?" I asked Beth.

She nodded, speaking between sniffs. "House both of them were born in. Officially a house but closer to a cabin in the woods. Mother is stranger than the two of them put together. Remember I told you, their mother intentionally only filled out one birth certificate. Officially Penn does not exist."

"Why?"

"So they could give each other alibis."

"She raised them to be criminals?" What kind of sick mother did these two men have? I guess I would never know the twisted beginnings of this pair but I was seeing the wrecked result.

"Yup, Ben loved me and was willing to leave all that. But I wasn't strong enough."

Who would be? I asked myself.

"Stop beating yourself up," I returned.

"So how much money and who is Penn involved with?" I asked

She put in a few more passwords and lists of names and locations popped up. Not what I wanted at this time, there were too many names. I wanted truth and justice for Beth. Crime rings were for the police.

"Why don't you email this to the police station?" I said. "I don't know what they can do with it, but can't hurt."

"Beth, just tell the police when they come to pick up Naomi that there is evidence of your brother-in-law and his associates on Ben's computer and leave it as it is." Josh commented from the door, and I didn't disagree. But my brain exploded at the thought of waiting for the police and filling out all the forms necessary to press charges.

I texted my husband several times again but no answer. He could be off watching a movie, but I didn't think so.

Chapter Twenty Five

Locked Ice House and a Stalker

After the police came and sorted out that Beth had a right to be in her house, Naomi was taken in to be booked for trespassing and assault on both Beth and myself. I could not believe how long this took and I was crawling out of my skin.

We left the house together as Beth did not want to be alone.

"So, Beth," I said as we stepped out in the frigid air. "How did Naomi find you?"

"She called me on my cell and I thought she was a friend. She was always nice to me—"

"Stop," I said standing completely still. "See that?" I was looking at an ice house with the door open and light spilling out. Silhouetted in the light was the dark shadow of my stalker.

Beth and Josh turned towards the lake. They then turned back to me.

"See what?" Josh asked.

I looked again and the door was closed, showing just the outline of light around it. The rest of the lake was silent and empty.

"Do you have an ice house?" I asked Beth.

She nodded.

"Take us to it," Josh said. Was he thinking the same thing as I was? Maybe Beth was on the lake for a reason before she got confused? I was still thinking about my husband and why my stalker was outlined with light. That was freaky.

Beth nodded and headed for a dark corner of the cluster of ice houses. The door was chained shut.

"I don't have the key," Beth said. Lady Friend started scratching the door with both front legs.

"Why is it locked?" I asked shivering. The wind was blowing out here. "None of the others seem to even have latches."

"Ben was like that," she replied. "They didn't want me in the ice house, so I didn't go."

We turned and started the cold shuffle back to shore when I heard thumping behind us. Beth and Josh didn't seem to notice. But Lady Friend was still whining and scratching the door.

I ran back to Ben's ice house. It was too cold to run, the air hurt my lungs. I didn't care. I kicked the door and I was sure I heard more thumping. Josh and Beth did not seem to notice I wasn't with them any longer. I kicked it again and it held. I tried to hit it with my arm but that caused a sharp pain to run up to my shoulder, so I kicked it again. Most ice houses are really just shacks and not very secure. Why was this door so tight?

I kicked the wall next to the door and it gave a little. I kicked it again and was able to push my foot through. Lady Friend was so anxious to help she was in the way. I used my good arm and pulled away a few boards. I was no longer cold. I was almost feverish in my determination to get into that ice house. I couldn't say why but I knew it was now or never. By the time I had bullied a small hole into the wall of the ice house, Josh and Beth had returned.

"Don't," Beth yelled. "Ben will be so mad at you."

I took a look at Josh, wondering what he was thinking. Beth was not really playing with a full deck.

Josh jumped in and helped me with a large chunk and I gasped. I could see a person, a large person tied up and still in the corner of the ice house.

I attacked the next board and it came off surprisingly easy. Inside was my sweet geek, unconscious with a huge note around his neck. It said, "Too late." I put my ear to his mouth to make sure he was breathing while Josh untied him. He was breathing but it was shallow and he did not respond to me.

I couldn't speak for the stiffness in my throat and chest. All I could do was cover him with my body and try to warm him.

"He's breathing," Josh said, grabbing my shoulders. "Easy, he's breathing."

I didn't answer. I just willed all my body heat to him and got as close as possible, wrapping my huge coat around us both.

Josh called an ambulance. They took forever but I couldn't seem to stop trying to get Kristoffer to respond to me.

I saw the reflection of cherry lights and I heard behind me people trying to get my attention. They couldn't have it. I was not giving up. Not for a second.

Kristoff blinked and smiled at me, and several large men in rescue overalls pushed me aside to put him on a gurney.

I don't remember getting him the hospital. Josh must have taken over. The next thing I remember is sitting in the waiting room and Josh giving me tea.

"What? No brandy?" I asked, my words slurring.

"How did you know to break into the ice house?" he asked.

"Lady Friend was upset and I heard thumps . . ."

A doctor walked by and I jumped up unsteadily to accost him.

"How is he?" I asked.

"Who?" the doctor replied.

I was momentarily stumped. It took me a minute to remember that an emergency room might have more than one patient.

"Kristoffer McCullum," Josh replied. Josh really was something of a rock even though he was a bit flighty—maybe I could consider him a partner.

"I'll check for you," was the vague reply.

"When can I see him?" I asked. I was persistent if nothing else.

The doctor turned away and I didn't hear the answer. I started to follow him.

"Hold on, Spitfire," Josh said grabbing my shoulders.

"You don't get to call me Spitfire, he does," I blubbered, suddenly overwhelmed.

The doctors had better let me see Kristoff soon. Otherwise I was going to make a fool of myself out here.

I sat down and rocked myself trying to be calm. I remembered that my husband had looked at me and smiled. He had to be alive. He had to be.

A young blond nurse walked up to me probably five minutes later, but it felt like forever as visions of life without my better half kept flitting across my mind.

"Are you Christine McCullum?" she asked. I nodded.

"Would you like to see your husband?"

I nodded.

Kristoff was awake in his hospital bed, smiling at me. His face was red and splotchy but his eyes were clear and his smile real although his lips were swollen and cracked.

"I'm so sorry," I said, running to him and trying to get all of him into my arms. He was too big for that, but I tried.

"It's me who should be sorry," he said, rubbing my back with his free arm. The other arm was hooked up to an IV.

"Thanks for finding me," he whispered.

I cried. I cried in relief and in gratitude and then I thought about my stalker.

The nurse interrupted my ruminating by gently taking me by the shoulder and sitting me down. "You may be suffering from shock," she said. "And you aren't using that arm, you should have that checked. I see people all the time who get injured and don't know it because they are so focused on the person most gravely hurt."

I nodded but all I said was, "I'm staying in this room."

"I'll send the doctor in," she replied.

"And where is my dog?"

She gave me a puzzled frown and left.

I started to stand but Josh walked in.

"I'm leaving now," he said. "I had to keep Lady Friend in my car, and I had to leave it running with a window cracked open to do that. I couldn't let her get hurt after she was such a hero. I'll take her to Mindy's house and I'll take Beth to a new safe house." He looked around and added, "Good thing for her she has money in the bank and I know more than a few good cops."

"How many of those do you have?" I asked thinking that he couldn't possibly have enough safe houses.

"Call me," he responded.

I shook my head, "My phone is toast."

"Use this one." He tossed me a cheap flip phone and I let it bounce off me. I really didn't seem to want to use my arm. "It has my number in the contacts," he said.

I picked it up, still not moving my left arm.

"Get that checked," he said.

"We won't be safe until this is solved," I replied.

"Yup, but sleep tonight."

"Here," I replied firmly.

Chapter Twenty Six

A Better Idea

I didn't notice the doctor or complain about a nice cast on my arm. Maybe it was the pills the nurse gave me. In any case, I woke up with my head on my husband's warm, moving chest and my butt in a hard chair. Every muscle hurt, even the one in my head. My brain momentarily wondered if it was a muscle, but I told it to shut up.

"Morning, Bulldog," he said quietly. "I was impressed how insistent you were even completely doped up."

"They let me stay?" I asked, but it wasn't a question. They obviously did.

"Not really, you just kept getting out of the bed they put you in and wandering over."

I sat up and could swear I heard my bones creaking. And he grinned at me.

"Not so easy once the pain meds wear off," he said. "Breakfast's coming."

That sounded divine.

A chipper nurse in a colorful smock delivered two breakfasts. The eggs were not soft, but they filled a hole inside.

"You know," I whispered. "Justice be damned, these guys are not going to leave us alone until they get their money and drugs."

"We have them?" he asked. His eyebrows lifted but his eyes were clear and directed at me. He wanted the facts and he wanted them now. Can't say I blamed him.

"No," I replied. "But I think they're in one of the lesser used ice houses. Beth couldn't get into her own ice house, so she must have put them somewhere. We know Penn is in Clearwater, at least was last night, so he may not know we found you in time."

"Nice guy," was his only response.

"Do you want to talk about it?" I asked, suddenly aware of my lack of bedside manner.

"Not much to say," he replied. "I remember being hit on the head and having moments of awareness, not much else."

I nodded and pushed the breakfast tray away and put my head back on his chest.

"I do remember hearing pieces of conversation," he continued. He was looking at the wall and running his hand through my hair. I turned my head sideways to stare at the same wall and just enjoyed being petted. I wondered if this was how Lady Friend felt when I just stroked her head while I was thinking.

"I remember someone saying put a SHA message out."

"What is a SHA message?"

"Don't know what they meant, but SHA-one certificates could be used to hide a message on the internet, in plain sight."

"How?" I had never met Penn, was he smarter than I assumed?

"A person could use verification data as a code or a coded message right on the SHA certificate on a website. The certificate wouldn't work anymore, so a regular search would just show an error or a warning about an unsecured webpage. Most people would navigate away, but if you knew what you were looking for, you could pull the certificate and find the message. Most of it is encrypted, but often the key is included. I think it was in 2008 that it was proven that a 'boomerang attack' can break it in an hour on an average PC."

"Pretty fancy," I said into his chest.

"Not really, for someone who has managed to stay off the grid for his entire life. The brothers could communicate basic messages but there would never be proof a second person even existed like there would be with a burner phone or an anonymous email address."

We both became silent, comfortable enough with each other not to talk. I fell asleep and when the doctor came in, she woke me.

She smiled when she moved, and she moved quickly. She was shorter than me, which is an accomplishment, and she was a hundred pounds if wet and clothed. Her smock was loose and flowed around her movements.

"You're exhausted and had symptoms of shock," she said to me. "You need rest and lots of sleep to recover."

I nodded.

"Your arm is in a cast because you fractured the radius have it checked by your regular doctor in a couple of weeks."

"Okay," I said.

"You," she said to Kristoffer, "are lucky to be alive. You have a mild concussion. You have a mild concussion, but no signs of frostbite despite a dangerously low core temperature. You also need rest and lots of sleep."

He nodded. There really wasn't time to respond fully to her as she moved on. "See your regular doctor soon and have him or her monitor your recovery. Otherwise, you are free to go," she said breezing towards the door. "Do you want me to tell your friends in blue outside?"

"Yes," he said.

"No," I said.

We looked at each other. "They'll take over and tell us to not do anything but hide," I said. "We could be hiding for the rest of our lives."

"How about we tell the truth and not hide, respectively of course."

I giggled. He was funny.

"Okay, I'll send them in, and a nurse will be by to remove your IV," the doctor said, and left.

First to knock was the FBI. They both had dark blue suits on with white shirts and red contrasting ties. Their military haircuts were identical and they were clean shaven. One was tall and slightly stooped, almost as if he was trying to join us short people. The second one was large. He was around six feet tall and a solid column from shoulder to hip. This continued down to his feet as he placed them apart enough to maximize balance. This guy was a fighter, the suit was just a cover.

"Hello ma'am, sir," he said. His voice grated like gravel. "I am Special Agent Moss and this is Special Agent Black."

"Black Moss," I said quietly with a small smile.

"Don't be impertinent, young lady," he snapped.

"Hey," Kristoff said. "We're not the bad guys here."

"And I am not all that young," I added.

There was silence as Agent Moss just looked at me through half open eyes. I was waiting for him to ask if I was a lady. Slowly his lips twitched at the corners and a half smile almost made it to the surface. Then he spoke again.

"Feisty," he said. "It's easier to deal with feisty victims, less gnashing of teeth and sobbing in the corner."

I decided not to take offense and try to cooperate. Why did I feel like there was an army of ants under my skin? I really needed to go do something. Anything.

"My first question," he said, "is what made you think your husband was kidnapped?"

I couldn't explain that a stalker outlined in light and a dog scratching on the door told me. He might lock me up and I didn't think I would be able to sit still for that.

I stared at him, trying to think of a reason he could understand. He looked away.

"If you're telling the truth it's easy, and you don't need to think," he said.

"I would not have gone out without telling her," Kristoff said. "She probably doesn't know why it bothered her I wasn't home."

I turned to him, what a genius!

"What he said," I replied. "We were looking at Beth's ice house and the dog went nuts," I continued. "They can smell things we can't."

"Okay, we'll let that go," Agent Moss said.

"Do I need my lawyer?" I asked. I really didn't think he was going to believe anything I said.

"Do you?" he responded.

I pulled out the old flip phone Josh had tossed to me and called Mindy's number by memory.

"Hey!" she answered. "I haven't heard from you, I was getting worried."

"I'm here at Hennepin County being questioned by the FBI. Do I need you?"

"Probably not, you haven't done anything illegal, right?"

"Not that I know of."

"Well, I'm not in court today, I could run over if you like."

"Please, we need a ride home."

Agent Moss walked to the door. Agent Black came over.

"Don't get paranoid because of my partner."

"He doesn't believe me."

"Not an easy story, but why don't you tell us why you're involved with criminals?"

"I am not involved," I said. "I have been asking some questions for Beth's attorney for defense, that is all."

"They don't seem to like that," he replied.

"Nope, guess not," I said not trusting myself to say anything else.

"Here's my card, if you feel like talking to me," he said and left with Agent Moss.

Josh came in next. Where was the nurse to remove Kristoff's IV so we could leave already?

"Hey, Spitfire and company!" he said. His voice was booming and happy. The more I spent time with him the more I realized he was an adrenaline junkie. This was fun for him.

"The Feds think I'm lying or crazy," I put in quickly. "How can you be so chipper?"

He shrugged, smiling at me with a big, goofy smile on his big, goofy face.

I smiled back at him, I couldn't help it. Maybe I was as crazy as him.

"I talked my buddies at the local station and they are willing to have extra patrols around your house."

Yup, I decided I was insane too, because I was not going to go home and wait for the cops to protect me. I didn't think I wanted to live that way.

"Better idea," I said. "Mindy is going to come pick us up and we are going to go home and pack a bag. Then you are going to pick us up on the corner by the woods and take us to somewhere safe with awesome computer access. We're going to track these guys our way."

Josh bounced on his heels. "You want me to make sure you aren't followed."

"Yup, and my car is in the shop."

"Where should we go?"

"Let's decide that later," I replied looking around. "This is the least private room I've ever been in."

We waited and waited. The clock seemed to be frozen at the same time. I was checking out the IV and wondering if I dared to remove it myself when a nurse finally wandered in with her clipboard. She removed the IV and had us sign a few papers and then all we had to do was wait for Mindy.

She bustled in ten minutes later, her hair mussed up and her face red.

"If those ineffectual asses out there in the hall try to talk to you, refuse," she said without a greeting.

I didn't think I had ever seen Mindy in her full lawyer mode before and I liked it.

"Thanks," I said. "I owe you a hot cocoa."

"No, you owe me a full bottle of good brandy and an evening of chocolate in front of the fire with a full story."

She was really upset.

"You are so right, maybe homemade soup with that."

She almost smiled.

"Let's go!"

We trundled out of the room. The same two FBI agents were there leaning on the wall. They watched her intently, following her movements with their gazes but didn't move.

Several police were also standing around. One of them nodded at Josh but other than that they were also silent.

Josh gave us a finger wave and headed out the back.

Chapter Twenty Seven

The Note and a Badass Lawyer

Mindy was all business and no talk as she loaded us into her minivan. As soon as we were on the road she turned off the radio and waited a minute.

It was silent except the sound of the wheels on the road and our breathing.

"Talk," she commanded.

"Mindy," I said. "You are a badass."

"Talk about what is happening," she responded. She looked like my Mindy, driving the minivan like a housewife except her hands were turning white she was gripping the steering wheel so tightly.

"You know the start?"

She nodded silently tightening her lips. "So, this is my fault?"

"No," I replied. "In spite of appearances, I can say no."

"Since when?"

"I hate to say no, but I can," I replied. "Beth didn't kill her husband, and the person or persons who did are not happy."

"Happy?" she asked turning to look at me.

"Not happy that I'm involved." I said quickly. "Please watch the road, it's still slippery. Don't want you to be without a car too."

"Without a car?" she repeated almost to herself and focused on driving and silence.

She pulled into my driveway slowly. "Your dog is at my house," she said very quietly. "Take her with you. She can protect you better than I can."

"Thanks," I managed. I could not remember a time that Mindy was annoyed with me. I didn't like it.

"Those FBI guys don't believe you could have saved Kristoff from a kidnapping without their amazing help, so they are questioning the entire report. I guess in their definition there is no kidnapping without a note. No proof you did anything but guess how to save your husband. They are looking for you to be the bad guy. Just warning you."

We got out the car shivering. The wind was bitter after the warm hospital.

"I'll walk Lady Friend over," was all Mindy said before backing up and going the short distance across the street to her house.

"I'll make tea," I hollered to the retreating van. She probably didn't hear.

We hustled into the house and out of the wind. It was good to come home.

On the kitchen table was a note. I didn't want to read it. But I walked up to it anyway. We stood together and I wrapped my arm around Kristoffer. The note said, "Return my drugs, or he dies slowly." It was printed in red marker like a child's printing.

Neither of us touched it, I just put my head on him and held tight. Kristoff was my rock. He was so much a part of me I would be incomplete without him. How do you tell someone who prints in red marker that you don't have his drugs? And what kind of sick mind breaks into a house and puts a note like this to be found when it's too late?

"We need to find those stupid drugs," Kristoff said. For a second I wondered if I should tell the FBI, but that was smothered by thinking about Agent Moss. He would probably accuse us of writing the note. He wouldn't look or help. He was sure we were in on something.

"Beth had them on the lake but didn't when she came off the lake," he said.

"But she couldn't get into her ice house."

"There's a whole city of ice houses," he reasoned.

"Tomorrow, let's take the dog for a walk on the lake," I responded.

"Good idea, but let's not spend the night here."

"Nope, let's have tea with Mindy then find a good hotel with internet that takes dogs."

He nodded and went to pack a bag. He didn't have to tell me, I knew that he would pack up his laptop and gadgets galore.

Mindy knocked once and let herself in. Lady Friend came in with a clatter of toenails. She sniffed me once and ran off and checked on Kristoff. Then she came back and greeted me again, wiggling and trying to sit but unable to stay still.

I just sat on the floor and pulled her against me until she settled. That required quite a face bath from a very insistent tongue.

Mindy stood by the front door. I met her eyes and she snapped, "Lock this stupid door."

I nodded not opening my mouth because I didn't want a French kiss.

I pushed Lady Friend's head away for a second and said, "I'll make some tea."

"I'll make the stupid tea," she replied, latching the door and stomping to the kitchen. "But no brandy, I'm working here."

She stopped talking and I knew she found the note.

"Hold on, Lady Friend," I said getting up. "Stay, please."

I swear she nodded her doggy head and gave me one last lick.

Mindy already had her phone out when I joined her in the kitchen.

I wandered over to the stove and put on water for tea. Mindy was going through a series of phone trees by the sound of it.

"Press one, one more time, damn FBI! You would think they didn't want to talk to people." she muttered to herself. Yup, she was going through those hoops they use so you don't have to talk to a real person.

"Have your stupid note," she finally said to the phone. "No one touched it."

She turned off her phone and looked at me, questioning. I shook my head—I've learned about touching evidence.

"Tea?" she asked, finally setting down the phone.

I nodded putting little bags into huge mugs. One had a friendly pumpkin design and the other one said, "Don't mess with Texas."

I waited. I didn't think I could process more issues if she was still mad at me. You just need at least a couple of friends who have your back no matter what.

"How did you know?" she asked. "Why were you looking for him before you knew he was kidnapped?"

"I wasn't sure," I replied. "I was worried, and Lady Friend was acting anxious and my stalker standing by the ice house . . ." I petered out as she was just staring at me, not saying anything or nodding or any of the listening noises we all pretend not to use.

"Hello?" I said.

"Okay," she said shaking her head. "We'll blame the dog. That always works."

"Blame?" I said my voice rising and my temper starting a slow burn. "That dog saved the love of my life. No blame!"

"Nope," she said and looked at me with a crease between her eyebrows. "That makes you angry?"

"Why blame?" I muttered.

"Well, I don't believe in coincidence and no one will believe you have a stalker, so that leaves the dog. They have amazing sensory skills we don't. Like smell and sound."

"I'm having brandy in my tea," I responded. I did not want to argue, and she gave herself something she could share with the FBI or whoever she called. And it could have been the dog—except for the thumps. Maybe I imagined the thumps and the stalker.

"I don't think I'm up to you being upset with me," I said deciding to be my blunt self.

"I am not upset with you," she returned. "Well, not exactly."

"What?"

"I am worried. I shouldn't have pushed you into helping Beth's defense."

"I can say no," I replied.

She just silently raised her eyebrows.

"Well, I can't seem to say no to helping," I admitted. "I have a well-defined sense of guilt."

Kristoffer came back into the kitchen with two packed bags. "Let's go," he said. "I see Josh's car over by the woods."

Mindy gave me a sudden hard hug and whispered in my ear, "Call me, I won't call you." I pulled back and watched her face intently. She shrugged. "Stay legal, but first stay safe." She gave me a tiny tight smile, "That is my considered legal advice." I hugged her back and turned quickly to head out the back door to the yard and our escape.

Chapter Twenty Eight

Offense on the Run

J osh's car was dark and silent. I opened the rear door and the overhead light didn't go on. We stumbled into the back seat with Lady Friend and a silent Josh started the car and started moving slowly. He drove around the lake and around several convoluted circles through quiet dark neighborhoods.

"Where are we going?" I finally asked.

Josh shrugged. "This is your game," he said.

"There are only two motels that take pets in this neighborhood, we can go to one of those."

Josh shook his head. "Too obvious."

"We need to search the lake in the morning."

"We need to make it to the morning."

"Fine, head to Clearwater," I snapped. "Penn is so sure we're terrified, that's the last place he'll look."

Josh nodded. The car roared into life and suddenly we were on the freeway going north slightly over the speed limit.

"I'll stay too," Josh commented over the rumble of the car. "We should be out on the lake with the sunrise."

Soon we eased into a dark parking lot attached to a darker motel that advertised vacancy and a willingness to take pets.

There was only one dim light on over the office and the lot was littered with beer cans and fast food wrappers. I think they had a willingness to take anyone or anything.

"Are you sure you want to stay?" I whispered. I don't know why I whispered except I was afraid a loud noise might blow the place down.

Josh nodded. "I've stayed here before. It's cheap but somewhat clean and it has internet."

I nodded. "You two stay here," he continued. "I'll check in." I nodded and Kristoff tried to hand him his credit card. "Nope," Josh said. "The attorney for the defense will be paying for this and we don't want your credit card followed. Put it away."

Josh parked under an overhanging tree around the back after registering and we scuffled into our two rooms. "No one else staying here tonight?" I asked looking at all the dark windows.

"They have more business in the summer and on the weekends," Josh replied.

Lady Friend was very interested in the many distracting scents and I let her check out the parking lot and the line of trees behind us. An hour out of the city is in the country in Minnesota. The snow was knee deep as soon as the trees started, and the only tracks were animal tracks.

Lady Friend and I had a nice game of catch the bean bag. She could jump really high and I liked to throw the bean bag as far and hard as I could. She always caught them. Then, while she sniffed every corner of the parking lot, I stretched, going through my beginner's form. I was learning self-defense because Kristoff nagged me into enrolling in classes after my last run-in with a crazy and violent man, but with all the excitement I'd missed a few classes. I doubted I would ever be able to use a roundhouse kick better than my pepper spray but it made Kristoff feel better. It wasn't long before the cold started to find ways under my coat so we went in.

Our room was as advertised. The bedspread was a faded flower print and there were stains in the bathtub and on the floor. But it was wiped clean and there was a desk with a lamp. Kristoffer had dropped our bags on the floor and he set his laptop on the desk.

"Show me SHA certificates and how they could be used to send secret messages." I said without preamble.

He nodded and was already hooked up to the internet. Guess I played with Lady Friend longer than I realized.

Josh was standing in the doorway. "What's a SHA certificate?" he asked.

"Come in and close the door," I replied. "We're about to find out."

Josh took the second chair and I sat on the bed.

"SHA is just a certificate level. Information can be put into a certificate inside the code so it's encrypted. This is a process that was designed by NSA but is now old technology. People tend to ignore it. I studied up on the 'boomerang attack' when it happened because I had to make sure our bank is secure from it. It's what I do."

"What are you talking about?"

"The certificate just contains information about who is behind the website and who is responsible for it, and it uses a third party to encrypt it so that it is known to be valid. In this case to use it as a code, the changes would make the certificate invalid so the page would show an error message or an unsecured site. As this happens quite a bit by accident, it's largely ignored."

"Humm," Josh responded his face crunched in his attempt to think clearly. "How would you find it."

"It will be hidden in plain sight."

"That doesn't help," Josh replied.

"Sure it does," I piped in. "Let me in."

I googled Ben's Real Deals. "I thought this website was weird when I first looked at it. So professional on one level and yet so incomplete."

I clicked on "Contact Us" and there was a message that the site was unsecured.

"That looks pretty normal to me," Josh muttered.

"Oh, yeah, I see what you mean," my better half agreed. "This certificate has been broken for over a year. And how hard is it to say we sell real estate and contact us at this phone number or this email address? Wouldn't you notice and fix that pretty quickly?"

I nodded. "But I don't understand how to see a SHA certificate or how to read it."

"Leave that to me," he replied, giving his hands a quick massage and then cracking them.

"Warming up?" Josh asked with his grin from ear to ear. I nodded and put my finger to my lips.

Josh nodded and lumbered to the door. "I'll get some rest, dawn will come soon."

To the soothing sounds of keystrokes, I took off my coat and boots and curled up under the covers. I was asleep in moments.

Morning found me wrapped up in a very warm body. He was snoring in my ear. Sweet but noisy. I managed to slip out without waking him and took a very long, very hot shower. Belatedly I hoped I hadn't used up all the hot water.

When Kristoff was taking his turn using up the hot water, there was tapping on the door in three knocks then a pause then two.

There was Josh, complete with a fast food breakfast and three huge cups of hot, bitter coffee.

"If I wasn't happily married," I said grabbing the coffee. "I would be seriously in lust over a man who wakes me up with coffee."

I grabbed a wrapped egg sandwich and started munching and burning the sleep out of my brain with scalding coffee. Josh joined me.

Lady Friend got an egg sandwich also as we had no dog food with us. We saved a sandwich for Kristoff and he joined us wet and wrapped in a towel.

"What did you find last night?" Josh asked.

"So much and so little," was his cryptic reply.

I narrowed my eyes and glared at him. Sometimes my manager glower helps. Not today. He winked at me.

"Seems Penn is pretty desperate to get back the money and drugs," he said.

"Not a huge revelation," I commented.

Kristoffer's eyebrows went up to where his hairline should start.

"But," he continued, "the reason is that they are not his drugs or money."

"Oh, shit," I muttered. This was a major break in my speech pattern as I don't swear or cuss. Well, I didn't before agreeing to help Josh with a few questions.

"Josh," he continued. "Do you have a way to get a message to the cops without having to go to the station and fill out forms?"

He nodded.

Kristoffer continued, "There is a reference to a friendly cop who will help them but no names. I don't think it would be a smart idea to trust them with our survival."

"Oh, shit," I repeated. That made Kristoff turn to me for a minute then start to chuckle.

"Your language has taken a turn for the worse," he commented and continued to chuckle.

"Well, shit," I replied. "Will finding the drugs and or money get us out of this mess?"

"No, probably not," he replied suddenly not amused anymore. His face looked drawn and tired now that he wasn't teasing. "We need to do that, but catching Penn is the only way to remove the price he has on your head.

"My head?" my voice rose at least an octave.

"Seems you have been a thorn in his side ever since retiring Ben."

"Retiring?"

"I think that is code for removing him from this plane of existence," Josh added.

"Got that!" I snapped.

Here I was getting two men I cared about in harm's way because I couldn't let Beth freeze to death. That just would not do.

"How about you two going into the FBI and showing them the messages and get their help?"

"Not without you," they said together. Wonderful, next they would start singing and dancing together.

"Let's go then," I returned stiffly.

"Let me get dressed first," Kristoff replied and started to put on his clothes. Josh ignored the show of the towel coming off and pants going on. I usually enjoy this part of the morning, but it felt unreal or like part of a nasty dream.

I took Lady Friend out to the parking lot to relieve herself and let her check out the amazing smells that survive the winter cold. I considered stealing Josh's car and going alone back to the lake, but there were no keys in my pocket and hotwiring a car is another skill not in my employee manual.

Within minutes, two men and our stuff were in the car and they were ready to rumble.

"That was fast," I snipped.

"I thought you wanted to be on the lake at sunrise," Josh responded.

Kristoffer sat in front with Josh and I cuddled with Lady Friend in the back seat. How I could solve this and keep them safe was the only thought on my mind the entire ride. It was dark and cold in the predawn light. I watched trees that were just dark shapes fly by through the window.

"I think Beth might be some help," I commented, and Josh nodded.

As Josh had dropped her off at the safe house, he knew where it was. In fact, any of the police at his old station would have known. Now that we knew there was a cop friendly with Penn, it didn't seem safe at all. I knocked at the door of the small blue house on a back street. It took three tries before a sleepy Beth in flannel PJs opened the door a crack and peered out at me.

"Morning!" I said trying to infuse cheer and enthusiasm into just a smile. I don't think it worked.

"What?" she responded, blinking in the light of a sun starting to show over the horizon.

"We're going to go looking on the lake for drugs and money," I replied still trying my sunshine smile on her.

She closed the door, almost hitting my nose with it.

I turned and looked at the two in the car and shrugged. Josh unrolled his window.

"Try again," he said. His breath froze on the way out of his mouth making frozen mist to be blown away by the breeze.

I knocked again, and silence was my answer.

I knocked again and the door flew open. "Fine!" Beth said in a sharp voice. "I'll come with you, but I'm staying in my PJs." She pulled on a sweater over her head and added a thick coat. Much smarter dressing than when I pulled her off the lake just a few weeks ago.

We came to the public access to the lake where I parked to find Beth. I looked around for my stalker, but he was never around when I expected him. The lake looked deserted, which was what we wanted for this search mission.

I didn't put a lead on Lady Friend. I wanted her to go where her instinct and sense of smell took her. We headed for the cluster of dark shacks. You would think that ice houses would be spread out evenly over the lake. But no, they cluster together. I think the fishermen congregate where the fish are biting. But it just looks like they don't want to be alone in one of the most solitary sports I know.

We shuffled, the sliding walk that works best on ice and I tried to think like Beth. Where would I go and where would I leave drugs and money if I had to run from fear? The closest ice house was two feet by three feet big. The door was closed but unlocked. I knocked and when answered by silence, I pushed the door open. A man was sitting on his bucket hunched over his hole in the ice. He turned his head to me with a frown between his eyes and tight lips.

"Sorry," I mumbled and backed out.

"Beth," I said my breath still making clouds of frozen mist. "Where would you hide something out here?"

"To hide and die if I was caught?" she finished.

"Yeah."

"It's all a haze of fear," she replied. "I came from that direction," she said pointing her mitten west, "and I was running," she looked around. Then shook her head. "I don't remember."

"You don't, or you don't want to?" Josh interrupted.

I frowned at him, but he didn't notice.

I looked at the hodgepodge arrangement of the ice houses around us and I thought I saw a shadow of someone standing by a hole in the ice with no house over it on the edge of the group. Was that shadow my stalker? Was he helping me or just annoying and around?

As neither Josh nor Beth were doing anything but glaring at each other and Lady Friend was busy sniffing each house, I headed for the hole with a stick to mark it. Some fisherman are too tough or cheap to have an actual shed over them. They just drill a hole, sit on their bucket and fish out in the open. It doesn't take long for a hole to freeze back up and this was not an exception. I could see where it was drilled and there was an indentation where a bucket had sat long enough to sink into the ice a little. Beth joined me and looked at the frozen circle.

"Is this it?" I asked her.

"Maybe," she replied. "I don't think I would go into someone else's ice house. I'm always scared of those little houses, even the ones with battery powered lights, they look so much like traps."

"Have to borrow an auger to get back into that hole," Kristoffer commented coming up behind me. "I'll go see if we can borrow one."

Sunrise found us drilling a hole in the ice. Sure enough, there was a plastic, sealed bag frozen into the ice. I didn't know what kind of drugs, and finally I was out of questions.

Beth was standing alone shivering and my hands were very cold inside my wet mittens by the time we dragged that wet frozen mess back to the car.

"Coffee shop," I demanded as soon as we started out.

"No," Josh replied. "We are taking this piece of evidence directly to the police station."

"Ugg," Beth responded. "Drop me off at the safe house, I don't ever want to go there again."

"Me too," I added. "Beth and I need to talk."

"Come on," I said to Beth jumping out of the car when we stopped at the light blue house. It looked cozy and warm with yellow light coming out every window.

She shuffled towards the door with her head down. "Now that we are turning Ben's drugs and money to the cops, what is going to keep us alive? They won't be pestering me to tell them anything, they will just want to get rid of me."

"Wait a minute," I said touching her, "Don't you mean Penn's?"

"No," she whispered. "My husband was the drug dealer, Penn was just muscle."

"How did Ben get killed?"

"I keep telling you, I don't believe he was."

"Who was murdered?"

"Penn," she whispered. "He had a temper and it was always getting him in trouble. I wanted Ben to give up the drugs but he couldn't."

"Couldn't or wouldn't?"

She shrugged. "I thought couldn't, but wouldn't might be more accurate."

"What will stop this?" I asked, really not expecting an answer. "And who is after you?" remembering I was also a target because of her.

"Ben's business contacts are angry I hid the drugs. I just wanted him to stop using them." She wiped her face with her arm and sniffed.

"Beth," I said. "Your lonely-hearts club is deadly."

She nodded getting to the door before me. "Time to pay the piper," she said.

That was an ominous thing to say. I stepped back and considered running back to the road. Maybe Mindy was right and it was the spouse. Just because Beth was in trouble didn't mean she wasn't the murderer.

We were not alone. There was Ben at the door. Yup, running was a good idea. I expected Beth to chase me and I was not pleased to be correct. She tried to grab my coat but I spun around and she missed. I ran off the driveway into the yard and the snow slowed us both down.

"You saved my life twice," Beth yelled. "Why?"

"I don't know," I replied, also yelling.

"Damn it," she said suddenly, dropping to sit in the snow. "He wants you here, but I can't fight you. You saved me. I can't fight him, I love him. I can't, I just can't."

"Beth," said a low voice. "You are a mess."

"They took the drugs to the police station," Beth said quickly to the shadow coming closer, her voice high and squeaky like a mouse.

Ben was tall and dressed in warm ski gear. He stared at her and walked slowly towards her as if he was trying not to spook her.

"Don't worry, my love," his low voice crooned keeping his eye on her. "This will soon be over." He had a small firearm in his hand and I almost choked looking at it. He raised it to her head and she just stared at it. I backed away. I should run, I told my brain, run and hide.

My hand found Lady's bean bag still in my pocket. Nope, I guess I was not going to listen to reason. I threw it at his head as hard as I could. It hit with a thud and knocked him off balance a little.

"Run, you fool!" I yelled at Beth. Ben turned slowly towards me and I wondered how I was going to live through the next few minutes. Beth kicked out and slammed her foot into Ben's leg. He looked down at her in the snow and I pulled out my canister of pepper spray. I ran at him, spraying and screaming in a guttural battle cry. I was going to fight for this life.

He shot his little gun at me but was off balance from Beth and a bullet tore through my coat. He took aim again and Beth kicked again. He shot down at her and she screamed. I got to him with my pepper spray and managed to get both eyes. I hit him on the head with my cast, screamed in pain, then hit him again in his face. He fell back in the snow yelling and I pulled out my new phone and dialed 911.

Ben thrashed around, his little gun lost in the snow where he dropped it. People who like to give pain don't seem to be able to take any was the thought that bothered to be in my brain at that moment. His hand was inching towards the gun even though he could not see well. I stomped on his hand and he yelled. So I did it again, and again. I kicked him everywhere he tried to move. I couldn't stop.

I was pulled away by strong arms and a wonderful scratchy voice.

"No more, Spitfire," was all my husband said.

I looked around and saw the cherry lights of the police and an ambulance. That is when I let go and started shivering wildly and crying.

Kristoff walked me over to an ambulance and I saw my stalker standing at the edge of the yard, watching and waving at me. Nope, I was not going to talk to him. I decided to ignore him, maybe forever.

Epilogue

Beth joined Mindy and me for tea with brandy in my kitchen. Well, no brandy for Beth. She was in treatment. Her arm was still in a cast from the shot she took but the real healing was for her soul to do. She needed to be independent and strong. Apparently, these are hard things to learn. She was seeing counselors and found religion. I was willing to be there to help but I was not willing to take any more heat for her.

Ben was in jail, as well as Andy, Naomi, and a cop named Seth, who was the head and brains of their little band. They never would have found evidence on Andy or the cop without the SHA certificates.

Apparently, the shortage in drugs caused by Beth's stunt had all of them in the cross hairs of some well-known but hard to pin down drug cartels based in Mexico. They were the heavy hitters, putting pressure on the twins and Seth. The SHA certificate method of communicating was theirs and it was not limited to this small operation. The SHA certificates gave the FBI more leads on the bigger target, once Kristoffer showed the cyber unit. This made the FBI very happy with us and apologetic for doubting me.

I agreed to be a part-time employee at Josh's PI firm. I like getting out and asking questions. It's the Customer Service Supervisor in me. Josh is intent on pushing me to get my own PI license.

Lady Friend was sleeping in her warm bed with her paws twitching in a dream.

"So," said Mindy. "Tell me about this stalker of yours."

I shrugged. "He is just always there when there's danger."

"Is he a good guy or no?"

"I don't know," I replied. "At first he scared the bejesus out of me, but he has never hurt me."

"Stalking is illegal," Mindy returned. "And dangerous people do it."

"He also gave me flowers," I muttered thinking. "You have to be real to give flowers, right?"

"What? You don't believe he's real?"

I shrugged. "Have you ever seen him?"

Mindy shook her head.

"Maybe you should see my shrink," Beth offered.

Wonderful was all I could think.

"Maybe," I said. But I didn't mean it.

They left together and I waved from my door as Beth got into her car and drove off and Mindy wandered across the street.

There on the corner was my stalker, just standing in reflected light, giving me a thumbs up. I nodded and he backed into the dark.

Wonderful, just wonderful.

Thank you for reading my book *Customer Service Can Be Deadly*. If you like it, a review would be greatly appreciated! Indie authors live and die by the reviews that honest readers like you provide.

And watch for the next book of this series, Customer Service Over the Edge coming soon to an Amazon near you!

If you would like notifications of my future mystery work, including the third book of this series, please sign up to my mailing list. I promise, no spam and no sharing of your email.

www.niche-publications.com/contact-us.html

If you have something to say and want to write a book to say it, I recommend SPS, Self-Publishing School. They will not only give you the invaluable technical help in just getting this stuff to work on the computer, but will be there for questions and even panic attacks. I don't think I would have done this without the guidance and encouragement they have given me.

Check it out:

https://xe172.isrefer.com/go/curcust/ Chrismckaypierce

Acknowledgments

It took a lot of help to finish this story! Thank you all! I want to thank Michelle Hill who created the cover for this hard copy! I want to thank Nancy Pile and Mandy Baxter, who were inspiring and patient editors, and Angelique Mroczka for her quick, professional formatting and her cool reason. A group of ladies with heads on their shoulders is an amazing amount of help! Thanks!

About the Author

The author lives with her extended family in Minnesota, with deer in her backyard and a hawk that torments her calico cat. Of late, the woods next to her driveway are being cleared to make room for more houses. Hope no bodies are found . . .

Chris has five grandchildren who provide hours of funny stories and fill her life. Three of them are close enough to visit by walking. She has worked in customer service and technical help for over 20 years. She is now writing full time and working at her daughter's liqueur store, TOASTED laughing and joking with customers and delivering locally.

Made in the USA
Lexington, KY
11 September 2018